Ken Lansdowne

A MURDEROUS BALL of FLUFF

A Bent Mystery
2

H Publishing
Denver, Colorado

Dedicated to:

CW Davis

He never had the chance to read this
But it would never have been finished without him.
You are so missed.

PUBLISHERS NOTE: This is a work
of fiction. Names, characters, places
and incidents are the product of the
authors imagination and are used
fictitiously. Any resemblance to
actual persons living or dead, events
or locals are entirely coincidental.

No part of this book may be
reproduced in any form or by any
means—including photocopying
or electronic reproduction—without
permission from the publisher.

Library of Congress Cataloging in Publication Data
The fairy dust killer: a novel/ Ken Lansdowne
    p. cm.
ISBN 0-9740853-3-0/978-0-9340853-3-3
1. Title.

First Edition/ 1st Printing 2009

Published by H Publishing
605 South Clinton Street
Denver, Colorado 8024

H Publising

Printed in USA

A MURDEROUS BALL of FLUFF

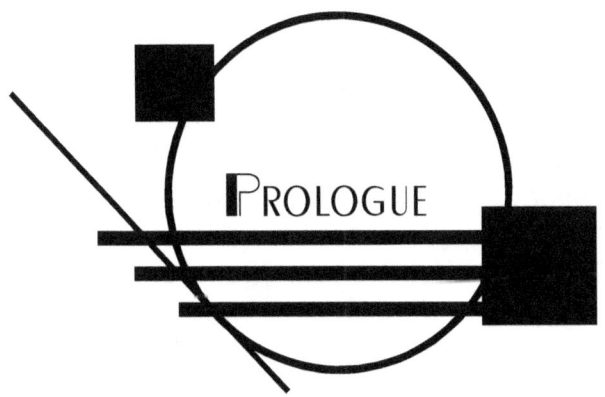

PROLOGUE

The light on JB's answering machine was flashing and the tape was running. The problem was there was no one at home to listen to the message being left.

zzzzzz....buzz......zzz....sss......."Sally, you have..... sss..."got to read"....zzzz......sss......"this new book" It is so"....click.....snap...zzz....."Why?..... zzzzz....."Did you fin"..sssss....zzzzzz.....sssss....click.....sssss...... buzz.......sssss.....click......sss......"But he's old"...... zzzzz......"Do we have to kill him?"....sss...."I don't like"...sss......zzzzz.....snap...."What if Harry decides to"...snap...zzz...click.......ssssss......zzzzzz..... zzzzzz.....ssss.......zzz.......click....ssss......."before he dies?.......ssss......zzzzz....."you'd get".......click.... zzzz.....zz....sss...."nothing".....zzzz.....snap....... ssssss........."but this isn't".......zzzzzzz...."what we".......ssssss...."planned"......zzz..click.... zzz......"didn't expect this"......zzzzz...ssssss... zzz.....click....zzzz........"damn auction"...."has ru-ined"......zzzzzz..."every"....buzz...zzzzz......"But murder!".......sss......snap...zzz....."Then you put in a"......."cup of flour"....zzzz...click....zzz..."Then the guy had the nerve"....zzzzz....click...zzzzzz....."Do you want"....ssss...."everything left"......zzz..."to his"....ssss....."foundation?"...."No, of course"...... zzz.... snap.......click.......sss....zzzz....click.... sssss......"but when?"...zzzz....sssss...zzzz..."will".... sss......snap......click....zzzzz.....sss."we do".... zzzzz...."it"....sssss....zzzz....."already start-ed".ssss.."it will be"..zzzzzz....ssss..."faster"... zzzzz....."soon."....click...."I slapped his".sss... zzz....."face"...ssss...click......"and......sss...... zzzzz.....sss...fold".zz.."don't"...sss......"stir"... sssss...zzzz.....click....sss..."so old now".....ssss........ zzzzz....buzz....zzzzz......sss....zz...."he'll die"....sss.... zzz.."anyway"......"this will".....ssssss..."be faster..... buzz......ssss......zzzz....

The machine ran out of tape.

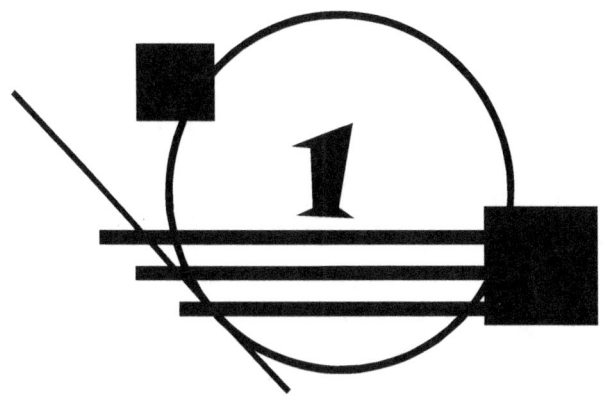

The key slid into the door of JB's apartment. It was a large apartment by New York City standards, having once been a small one-bedroom plus a studio on the lobby floor of the building. The obstructing wall had been removed when Jeremy Bent—known as JB to most everyone that he cared to know—moved from the West Side into Toby's apartment shortly after they decided to become lovers.

JB was a writer of mystery novels. Also his first stage play was currently in production for Off-Broadway. Toby, JB's companion, was Toby Gallo, younger than JB by a decade or two, and as handsome as a fifties movie star. He was also the owner of the three story six unit East 60's apartment building they lived in now that the previous owner, Toby's father, had left the country to live in Italy.

Along with JB and Toby was Len Matthews. He was around the same age as JB, give or take a prevarication or two, and lived on the second floor of this same building. He was a reasonably well known actor with ragged around the edges matinee idol looks, a head full of beautiful mahogany hair, and shoulders that once were broader than his waist but were now about even. He was JB's previous lover from a few years before and had hung around to become his closest friend.

It was a part of JB's character that people—including ex-lovers, old boyfriends, and even a couple of casual dates—once becoming a part of his life would stay. This guaranteed that come Christmas he received copious amounts of cards from people he had known since grade school on up.

JB opened the front door and stepped in. Then he took a step to the side and made a gesture right out of a Alexander Dumas novel—a foot forward, one bent knee, a bow at the waist and a sweep of his arm as if he carried a plumed hat. This extravagant gesture escorted Len, followed by Toby, grandly and somewhat sarcastically into the room. Len walked by and said, "A move worthy of the great....at least, according to you....director, Mr. Dalton Hughes."

"You're right, Len. He is the director. The only director hired by the investors in my play *The Greenhouse Murder*. So what he says is what goes."

"But he's a jerk, JB."

"He just happens to be the best theatrical director currently available. He won an OBIE, for God's sake."

Toby, who so far had kept his silence, now spoke up. "Listen, I've been listening to you two argue about this for over two hours now. Stop it, both of you, or I'm going to pull out every hair on my head."

JB looked at him. "Well, that sounds really painful....and quite unattractive."

"And every hair on your head is next, Mr. Bent."

Len smirked. "Toby, if you do that, at Halloween you could both put on yarmulke's, stand together, and be Dolly Parton's cleavage."

The two men stared at Len. He smiled back.

JB shook his head. "You are a very strange man, Len Matthews."

"I just happen to have a very active imagin...."

"Oh, crap! This thing is on the fritz." JB punched his finger at the buttons on a small plastic box next to his telephone. "The light won't stop flashing."

"On what?"

"My answering machine. It's saying I have more than a hundred messages."

"Mr. Popularity, aren't you."

"Hell, I'm not sure I even know a hundred people who are still talking to me."

He pushed a button, which caused the tape to whirr as it rewound. Then it automatically played back.

"What in hell? These aren't phone calls. This is all pops and static. And little bits of conversation. What's going on? This is weird."

"I'll bet I know," Toby said. "There's been a crew of telephone repair men on the block for the last few days now. They probably got your phone lines crossed with some others and the machine picked that up."

"Do we have to kill him?"...., the machine said.

"What was that?" JB hit the rewind button and replayed that section of the tape. "My God, I can't be hearing what I think I am?"

"Play it again, JB. That couldn't have actually said what it sounded like. Could it?"

"......."kill him?"....sssssssss...."damn auction".... ssssss.... sss..... zzz...."has ruined".....buzz.....ssss", the machine repeated.

JB looked oddly at the machine. "I can't believe I actually heard two men planning to kill someone."

Len said, "Admittedly that's what it sounded like. But, come on, JB. It was just a little bit of conversation. It could have been a joke or something."

"Len, when was the last time you joked with anyone about killing someone?"

"Wasn't it about an hour ago that I last threatened you?"

"Well, that bit of taped conversation did not sound funny. That was a real murder being planned, and we've got to do something."

"Oh, good God! Here we go again. JB, this is New York City. There are....as a conservative estimate.... eight or nine million people here. And you think you can find these two people out of all of them? So you can prevent something that probably isn't even happening?"

"He has to try, Len." Toby walked over to JB and put an arm over his shoulder. "That's why he is who he is."

"Then you're both delusional!"

JB said, "Len, I mean it, we have to do something. How could you live with yourself knowing that someone, another human being, is going to be killed and you did nothing to try to stop it? Not only is it morally suspect but it's totally unconscionable.

Besides, it'll be fun."

"No, JB. Dinner with Nathan Lane would be fun. Lying in bed with Bert and Ernie might be fun.... then I could find out if those damn puppets are gay. I know they've denied it, but....come on....twenty years in the same bed. There's something going on there." He waved a hand. "But I digress. To get back to my point. Even washing my unmentionables would be more fun than what you have in mind."

"Good God, Len, you are such a grouch lately. Why don't you go to a meeting?"

"I did. This morning. That's partly why I'm a grouch. I want to drink and I can't. Something else that isn't fun."

"But you can." JB pointed toward a gathering of liquor bottles on the kitchen counter. "There's plenty of alcohol right there. Help yourself. I'm beginning to think I'd prefer you that way over this."

Len gasped. "Sometimes you can be such a shit!" He headed for the door. "I'll talk to you when you decide to apologize, Jeremy Bent."

He walked out the door, closing it firmly.

"Uh-oh. He is pissed. He never calls me Jeremy except when he's really angry."

"Well," Toby said. "You were pretty hard on him. just now. Getting sober isn't such an easy thing to do, JB. It's work. Hard work. He's having what AA calls mood swings.

"Then I'll buy him a trapeze for Christmas. What I do know is he's been impossible for days now. Just a real pain in the ass. I mean, everybody at the theater is...."

It all started when Len disappeared from his usual haunts one evening several months ago. He was discovered the next day as a live-in patient at Payne-Whitney Hospital's rehab clinic.

A month later he came out of there changed. Not that he wasn't the same person, but now he was forced to deal with the world without the haze that his boozing had provided.

Giddy with his newly won sobriety, he was riding, as AA put it, on a pink cloud. He threw himself wantonly into the business of being sober. He went to meetings once, more often twice, a day. He swallowed gallons of coffee with his fellow members. He picked up ashtrays and coffee cups after meetings. He got a sponsor and called him every day as he was told to do. He was that season's AA poster boy. Then came the tumble off his colorful cloud as sober reality set in with a vengeance.

First, he had read JB's playscript. He knew the lead was perfect for him. Then, he began wheedling and whining for an audition. And, finally, on bended knee, he out and out begged JB and the director for the chance to play the part of the older detective in the Off-Broadway production of his play *The Greenhouse Murder*.

His begging actually got him the role. And that's when reality delivered its slam to his solar plexus. Len found that he was expected to pull out acting skills that had not been in use for quite a while. Skills that he had to find inside himself or not call himself an actor anymore.

The drinking Len had indulged in had closed doors throughout the industry. Especially the doors of the all important casting directors. So this chance to perform in a new play represented his entrée back into the only profession he knew and loved.

But like any play, rehearsals had been hard. On all of the cast and crew. But Len especially. There had been rewrites, cast changes, and technical problems. The intense pressure had gotten to Len. He had reacted to it by reverting to his very old and very destructive behavior.

Newly won sobriety wasn't only hard for the ex-drinker. His loved ones—and sometimes even complete strangers—got to suffer too.

THE GREENHOUSE MURDER
ACT 1, scene I

IT IS NIGHT. A LOW MIST FLOATS ALONG THE GROUND. AS THE LIGHTS SLOWLY COME UP WE SEE, STAGE LEFT, TWO POLICE OFFICERS IN SIL-HOUETTE.

BEHIND THEM, HOVERING LIKE A GREAT BEAST ABOUT TO DEVOUR THE OFFICERS, IS A GLASS GREENHOUSE STRUCTURE. IT IS LIT FROM THE INSIDE AND IS THE MAIN LIGHT SOURCE FOR THE OUTSIDE AREA.

LIGHTS COME SLOWLY UP ON THE POLICE-MEN WHO ARE LOOKING DOWN FROM A DIRT AND ROCK RISE ON WHAT APPEARS TO BE A DARK LUMP DOWNSTAGE FRONT. IT IS A BODY.

OFFICER 1

God. He's dead all right. His head's been crushed in. And just thrown away. Pretty bad, ain't it?

OFFICER 2

It's never good. This one's just a kid though. Can't be more than seventeen. What a shame.

OFFICER 1
(LOOKING AROUND)
Have you seen them guys from homicide? They was supposed to be here already.
OFFICER 2
They're here. Inside the greenhouse, talkin' to the owner and those two other guys.
(HE POINTS IN THAT DIRECTION)
OFFICER 1
Oh fine. And ain't that the way of the world? They're inside where its warm and we're stuck out here in the cold makin' sure a body that'll never move again doesn't right now.
OFFICER 2
Quit your grousin'.
(HE LOOKS BACK)
And look lively. Here comes someone now.

THE "SOMEONE" COMING IS A TALL MAN IN HIS THIRTIES. WELL PUT TOGETHER....EVEN DAPPER, WELL DRESSED, SLENDER, WITH MATI-NEE IDOL LOOKS. HE WEARS A TRENCHCOAT, BELTED. AND NO HAT. HE WALKS TO THE SPOT WHERE THE OFFICERS STAND.

1ST. DETECTIVE
(SPEAKING TO SOMEONE BEHIND HIM)
So, boy-o, we'll have to talk to each of the suspects, then. What are there? Three that we need to see. Oh, officer, where can I find....

(HE SPINS HIS ARMS AS HE STEPS
BACK FROM THE EDGE OF THE
RISE WHERE THE BODY LIES BELOW)
Wow, that's quite a drop. So this is where the kid got it? Not a pretty ending, was it?

ANOTHER MAN COMES UP BEHIND THE
FIRST DETECTIVE. HE IS YOUNGER—IN HIS MID-
TWENTIES—HANDSOME, WITH AN EAGERNESS
THAT MAKES HIM ENDEARING. HE IS DRESSED
THE SAME—A BELTED TRENCHCOAT WITHOUT A
HAT.

                    2ND DETECTIVE
But we don't know who the....
               (HE STOPS WHEN HE SPOTS
               THE BODY. HE STARES DOWN
               AT IT...STRICKEN)
My God! His head....It's....
          (HE PULLS HIMSELF TOGETHER)
I didn't expect it to look so brutal.
               1st DETECTIVE
     (WISE TOO THE WAYS OF THE WORLD)
Murder is never pretty, kid. He'll look better
when they get him downtown and clean him up nice
and neat.
               (ALL BUSINESS NOW)
What we have to do is check out the scene and
figure out what happened. Right, officer?
                    OFFICER 1
Just who in hell are you anyway? I don't know
you. You're not from this precinct.
               1st DETECTIVE
You're right. I'm not. The name is Gallent. Gray
Gallent. I'm a private dick. I mean I'm a detective....
licensed by the state, and hired by the owner of the
greenhouse to find out who did this poor kid in.
This....
          (INDICATING HIS ASSISTANT,
          WHO ISN'T WHERE HE POINTS)
....is my helper. Joey Hil....ton....
               (LOOKING AROUND)

GRAY (cont.)
Where are you, kid?
                    JOEY
          (HE HAS MOVED DOWN THE
          RISE TO WHERE THE BODY LIES)
Here, Gray. Look at this....and its lying right next to the body. It must be the murder weapon.
                    GRAY
What? Don't move anything. Leave that where it is. There might be prints.
          (HE MOVES FORWARD AND
          LOOKS OVER THE EDGE OF
          THE RISE)
What did you find?
                    JOEY
It's a hammer, Gray. And it's covered in blood. Not very smart of the killer to leave it here.
                    OFFICER 2
But that's what you're going to do, boy-o. Homicide don't want the area disturbed.
                    JOEY
Right you are.

          (HE STANDS AND STEPS BACK,
          KEEPING DISTANCE BETWEEN
          HIM AND THE BODY)
But it doesn't look like there was any struggle, Gray. The ground isn't disturbed. And there isn't much blood here. The killer probably threw the kid down here after he was dead, and then threw the hammer after him just to get rid of it.
                    GRAY
Well, that explains the pool of blood inside the greenhouse. It's just too bad the building wasn't locked. With no lock on the door it could be anyone around here who did this.

OFFICER 1

Yeah, all the kids in the neighborhood use this place to get together. It's where they all hang out. They're always here. Smokin' cigarettes. Meetin' their girlfriends. You know...kid's stuff.

GRAY

Somehow killing a seventeen-year old boy doesn't seem like kid's stuff. You work this beat? Did you know the kid?

OFFICER 1

I work the beat, sure. But I don't know who the kid was. He's not one of the regulars. Probably not from this neighborhood.

GRAY

(TO HIMSELF)

Then what was he doing here?

(TO JOEY)

OK. We have three suspects. The guy over there. He's the greenhouse caretaker. Then the handyman for the apartments next door, and there's the lady that lives in one of the apartments.

JOEY

(HE MOVES UP THE RISE TO
STAND NEXT TO GRAY. HE PULLS
A NOTEBOOK FROM HIS TRENCH
COAT POCKET AND READS FROM
HIS NOTES)

OK, the guy over there,the greenhouse caretaker. He has a previous record. He's just out of jail on what he claims was a bum rap. But don't they all?

(HE TURNS STAGE LEFT)

The guy over there, the handyman. He's new here. Only been in the U.S. a few months....from Poland.... and still has those old country prejudices and fairytale beliefs. Silly supersitions. That sort of thing.

JOEY (cont.)
(FACES TOWARD GRAY)
And the lady next door is one of those mystic types. You know, believes in ghosts and mediums and other spooky stuff. A real nutcase. So, what'll we do about them, Gray? We question each of them, right?

GRAY
Yeah, but we don't want to alarm them, kid. So we'll do it on the sly. Know what I mean?

OFFICER 2
What I mean for you two is to move on. You'll both be in trouble if you hang around here messin' in our business. Homicide won't like your being....

THE LIGHTS FADE ON THIS SECTION OF THE STAGE.

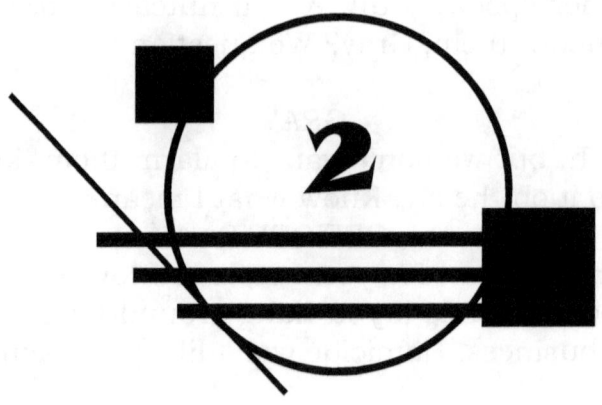

After an hour and a half of tediously transcribing the answering machine tape JB sat back in his chair.

"OK," he said. "Now we can see what we have." He looked directly at Toby and said, "It looks like these two men on the tape are planning to kill somebody named Harry because he's selling his things at auction. So the proceeds can go to his foundation. Now, I'm assuming here, but it looks like one of the men won't get anything out of the will when this Harry person dies if he does sell everything. That would mean he has to be pretty close to this Harry if he's mentioned in the will." JB pondered a second. "So, they....That is the man who stands to inherit and this someone else, are going to kill Harry before everything is gone."

"And don't forget that Sally has to read a book, and you're supposed to fold not stir," Toby added. "You know, JB, Len, amazingly enough, could be right here. This might be too daunting a situation to get mixed up in. Maybe we should call the police?"

"They wouldn't care. You know the old story, no crime has been committed so they can't do anything." JB rubbed his hands together. "So, what do we do first? I think we should find out who Harry is. Right?"

"Gee, that sounds easy. What are there, maybe thirty-two thousand Harry's in this neighborhood alone?"

"Well, we know our Harry has money." Toby looked skeptical. "He has a foundation. You don't have a foundation without having some major bucks somewhere."

"OK. That makes sense. But where do we start?"

"If this Harry person is having an auction, then there must be a pre-showing. So, I think going to the auction houses is the best way to find who's selling what."

"Your logic just got shaky. I think that if Harry has his own foundation he would probably be on the board of directors. So, if we look into all the foundations in New York that have someone named Harry as one of the members or the head of the board, we'll have our man. The library should have a listing of all the foundations in Manhattan and their current board members." Toby smiled. "Now that's a piece of logic even Mr. Spock could get behind."

"But it's not nearly as interesting or as much fun as my way. Besides my way could get me out of trouble with Len. There's nothing he likes better than shopping. Shopping has become his favorite vice since he stopped drinking."

"Well, you go shopping to find your Harry your way and I'll go to the library to do it mine. We'll can meet later and compare notes. OK?"

"I don't know if I want you doing anything at the public library. It's a notorious place to pick up indigent bibliophiles and you have a definite weakness for men of letters."

"I promise you, I'll watch my P's. But, you'll have to watch my Q's yourself."

"Its not only the Q's I worry about, it's the P's too—as in predatory old queens. That's what I worry about."

"Now whatever makes you think I'm going to be attracted to any other old queen than the one I'm already hooked up with?"

"Ouch!" JB hands covered his chest. "Bullseye. I guess I deserved that since I left myself wide open. But I do think you've been hanging around Len way too much lately. That remark was up to his mean-spirited standards any day."

"Well, we do spend a lot of time together at rehearsals, and you have to admit he does have a quick mind."

"Yeah, like a bear trap. I know people that have chewed their foot off at the ankle to get away from that mouth of his."

"Well, right now he's up in his den trying to soothe his hurt feelings."

JB hurrumped. "Len Matthews wouldn't know a feeling if it came up, tapped him on the shoulder, and introduced itself."

"JB, he's been putting a lot of feelings out on that rehearsal stage every day. And good ones too."

"OK. You're right. Despite all the trouble they've had, even Dalton says he's excellent in his part. If Len would just listen to Dalton instead of...."

Toby put both hands over his ears. "Stop it! I've heard enough of this already. Go upstairs and apologize to him right now and get this silly bickering over with."

"All right. But don't I always?" JB and Toby lightly kissed. "I'll talk to you later."

At the doorway to Len's second floor apartment JB hesitated a moment. Len is the one person in the world that I want to see get his life together, he thought to himself. After years of watching him, like Godzilla in downtown Tokyo, destroying everything in his path—including the lover relationship we used to have—he and I have finally come to a place where we can rest. This leap he's taken toward living his life, instead of constantly tearing it apart, has given us some hope for the first time in years. So, if it means I have to stand by while Len clings to this emotional roller coaster he's on then I'll have to pay my two bits and go along for the ride.

JB pushed the doorbell. Len opened his door and the two men stared at each other a moment. Len opened his mouth to say—Before he could JB said, "I'm sorry." That instant "I'm sorry." also came from Len's mouth. They smiled. After an apologetic hug they moved inside the apartment.

JB then explained to Len what he was able to figure out from the bits of conversation on the answering machine tape.

Len said, "You know, JB, I'm really not trying to rain on your little sleuthing parade here. If I can help I will."

"Great. I really can use your help. How would

you like to go shopping?"

"Would Cleopatra kiss an asp? Why? Was there some sort of Bloomingdales connection I missed?"

"You know, Bloomie's isn't the only place to shop in New York City."

Len's jaw dropped. "You have just spoken sacrilege, you infidel. Move out of the way before the angry bolt of lightening turns you to a large charcoal briquette."

"I'll take my chances here. What I figure is if this Harry person is having an auction then you and I should be able to find out who he is at any of the auction houses scattered around Manhattan."

"Oh, I get it. A safari. Let me get my pith helmet out of moth balls. But, your idea is a pretty good one, JB. Anyway, I've been looking for the perfect armoire for that wall over there. And you can get bargains at auctions. OK. I'll go with you. Lead on, Miss Marple."

"How many times do I have to tell you, Len. I look terrible in tweed. Can't you find another detective's name to use."

"OK. How about Scobby-doo?"

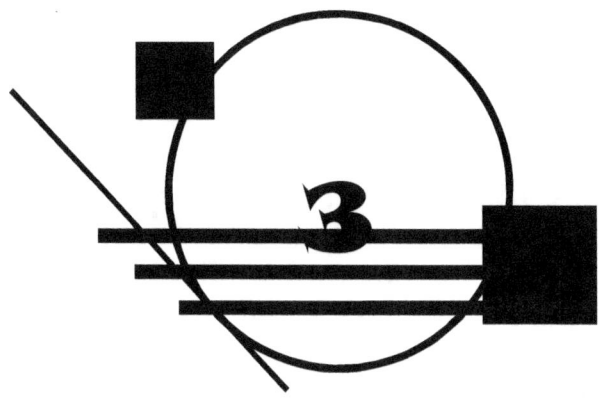

While Toby walked up the steps of the Main Branch of the city library on Fifth Avenue the lounging granite lions on each side looked balefully upon the people passing by, as if poised to swipe with sharp talons at the next person who caused the street traffic to honk and interrupt their repose.

Inside the building all was dark woods, heavy air, and weighty quiet. At the information stand a woman who looked as dry and crumbly as a snack cracker directed him to the reference floor across the street in the library annex.

Deciding not to chance a lion's angry claw he crossed at the corner light. Walking past the souvenir shop on the left of the revolving doors and to the central bank of elevators, Toby began to feel himself relax. The annex was more a jeans, shirt and casual jacket kind of place.

Upstairs Toby headed for the information desk that stood directly in front of the elevators. This time it was a rather attractive twenty-ish blond man behind the desk, his shoulders hunched over a pile of papers.

Toby checked and approved of the librarian's looks, but then felt a twinge of guilt, as if JB had some way of knowing he'd checked out another man. JB's constant problem with jealousy had become very old, very fast, especially considering that Toby had given him no reason to act that way. Just because Toby checked out someone else's ass occasionally didn't mean he was going to run off with him any time soon. But if JB persisted in these silly suspicions—well, one never knows, do one?

The librarian cleared his throat.

"I'm sorry." Toby said. "Could you direct me to the section on foundations, please?"

The man removed his glasses. "Would you be referring to the word 'foundations' as in building materials. Or do you mean 'foundations' as in benevolent institutions?" He was bored. His voice was saturated with it. But then, as he finally took notice of who was in front of him, the man's eyes wandered down his body like Toby was an all-you-can-eat buffet. He replaced his previous tone with something a bit more unctuous. "You know, you look just like...."

Here it comes, Toby thought. The usual comparison to Montgomery Clift. My whole adult life people have told me I look like the famous actor. Even now, after Clift has been dead for umpteen years. Not that I mind all that much. Good-looking people do seem to get better treatment in this world, and I'm not going to turn down any chances that might come my way. But, as an actor, I'd rather be known for being more than just pretty. I have other things to offer too, not just my looks.

The librarian continued. "....like a friend of a friend of mine. Are you Fred Morris?"

"Huh? Oh. No, I'm not. Sorry," Toby said, regaining his grip on reality. The voice inside his head went, OK. So you misread the guy. Not everyone you meet is on the make, you conceited idiot. Outloud, he said, "But I mean foundations as in institutions. Where can I find them?"

The librarian smiled again. "I would be happy to show you where they are. Just give me a moment and I'll be right with you." The librarian's smile had taken on all the attributes of a leer as he evened out the stack of papers in front of him.

Toby's inner voice shouted triumphantly, Ah-ha! I wasn't wrong after all. Here comes the come on. Shaking his head, Toby said, "That won't be necessary, thank you. I don't want you to get behind in your work."

"Oh, this? Don't worry. It won't be the first time I got behind...." He paused, his leer transforming into something more salacious. Saliva practically dripped from a corner of his mouth. "....if you know what I mean," he finished.

Toby sighed inwardly. "No, thank you," he said, using a tone that left no doubt about what he actually meant. "Directions will be just fine. I can find my own way."

The clerk, with obvious disappointment, put his gonads back where they belonged, and gave him the directions. Toby smiled nicely and followed them to the designated destination.

He found the section, then found the correct Dewey numbers, and then found a thick book named *Foundations and Philanthropic Institutions of the Greater New York Area, Including Its Boroughs.* Well, you can't get much closer than that, he thought.

He pulled the book from the shelf and headed for a table. He put the book down and took a seat. The book was about three inches thick and had print that was as small as a Grinch's heart. Toby sighed and began to read.

Len turned back to talk to JB. "Will you catch up?"

"Not as long as you've got that thing," JB answered.

Len looked down and spun around. "What thing?"

"That thing hanging off your shoulder. What the hell is that?"

You mean my bag? I need some place to carry my stuff."

"Well, why don't you use a backpack like any other decent New York fairy. That looks like a purse. Like a really big purse."

"It is....I'll have you know....a Tarina Rose shoulder clutch. It's very chic. And very expensive."

"It is, no matter how you fancy it up with pretty names, a purse. And we queers haven't worn purses since the seventies. And even then we told people we were photographers and not just silly affected queens."

"Well, affectation or not, I like it. So I'm wearing the bag."

"All right. But if anyone calls you ma'am it isn't my fault."

They started walking again, headed toward York Avenue, where the auction house was located,

Just as they started thinking they were going to run out of island and would need to tread water the door to Sotheby's came into sight.

JB and Len pushed through the entrance onto the light colored marble floors of the lobby. There was a wood veneered coat check booth directly in front. On the right were three polished wood steps leading to the galleries. These galleries were showrooms that held the goods coming up for auction in the next few weeks.

They turned and headed toward the steps. A guard, previously standing beside the coat check booth, came up behind Len, stopped him, and quietly said something to him.

"What do you mean I have to check my bag?" Len's voice had a distinct snap to it.

"I'm sorry, sir, but all bags have to be checked."

Venom now filled each of Len's words. "Then why is that lady carrying her bag?" He pointed to a woman who had entered just ahead of JB.

"But that is the ladies purse, sir."

Len had now graduated to outright malevolence.

"And how, pray tell, is that woman's purse any different from my shoulder clutch?"

The guard's face had by now taken on a pink glow of discomfort. He turned toward the coat check and held up a single finger for reinforcements. The young woman inside the booth looked to her left and almost immediately a door beside the booth opened. Another man, wearing a suit and tie instead of a uniform, moved purposefully, even a bit menacingly, across the floor.

He stopped opposite the guard and Len. They were now all three standing, alone, on a tiny island left to them by the other people in the lobby.

Len looked over to JB, who held up his hands in an *I'm not getting involved—you're on your own* gesture. He turned and walked away from Len and up into the galleries.

Down a long hallway to the right was the main reception area. This was dominated by a massive half-curved desk. Behind it were rows of paperbound catalogs of current and recent auctions sitting on dark wood and brass accented shelving. A flower arrangement of twigs and orchids standing as tall as a man rested on one end of this behemoth of a desk. The entire area had the feeling of a continental hotel lobby in all of it's decadent splendor.

JB stepped up and asked the *this is my first job in the city, and I just got my degree in Fine Arts, and isn't being an intern just the neatest* receptionist if there was anyone with the name of Harry, or something similar, having an auction in the next few days.

The girl quickly, and actually quite efficiently, checked through her catalogs, looked up, and answered in the negative. Then she gave him a blinding white full-toothed pink-gummed dentist-enhanced smile. No one should be allowed on the streets with that much perky, JB thought to himself.

Resisting an urge to grab the girl first by her forehead and then by her chin and crunching everything in between like a bag of potato chips, JB thanked her and headed for the lobby. The whole operation took only three mildly irritating minutes.

Len was still in the center of the lobby, holding his ground like an Armani suited Barbara Frietchie, having his confrontation with the security staff. JB got his attention, indicated he was ready to leave and went outside.

A few minutes later Len came out swiping at imaginary dust on his lapels. "You'd think they would be a more civilized? Well, let's go to Christies. They should be better. They are British after all."

"Sothebys is a British company too, if you must know. And you can't blame them, Len. That bag you're carrying is enormous. So, you may as well expect to check it at any and all of the places we're going to today, all right? I will not spend the afternoon watching you argue with every security guard in every auction house we go into."

"I'm just doing my bit for gay rights, JB. Why should a woman with a purse be allowed to carry it when I can't carry this? Answer me that."

"Since that 'clutch', as you call it, is big enough to hold a Chippendale chair I think they have a point. Not that I don't agree with you in principle. But making sure some expensive something doesn't disappear into a clutch is their job, so you may as well get used to it."

JB started to walk away.

"Well, all right. But I don't know how I'm supposed to hold my head up high at the next gay parade."

Having worked his way to the D's, Toby was pretty sure he has found the Harry he'd been looking for. A cross check in *Who's Who In America* confirmed it.

A photocopy from the relevant page of each book, and a prayer of thanks that Harry's last name didn't begin with an X, allowed Toby to bid a fond farewell to his horny librarian.

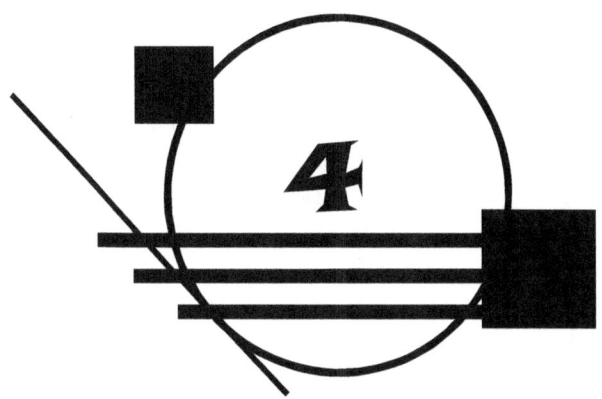

The rest of JB's and Len's afternoon had been spent visiting the six or seven auction houses between 73rd and 87th Streets on the Upper East Side. Dragging four tired feet they finally turned onto 87th Street and aimed for the last house on their list.

"Are you going to haul me into every flea infested storefront that shows any old saggy sofa in a window?"

"No, Len, I promise this is the last one we have. So quit your bellyachin' and we won't have to lallygag here anymore than necessary."

"I swear, Jeremy Bent, sometimes you use the cutest Southern expressions. And you're not even from the South. At least when I use them I come by them honestly."

"Sometimes I use Yiddish expressions. It doesn't make me Jewish."

Once inside the lobby of the auction house JB bent to look at a rack of catalogs. He picked one up, read the cover and put it back. "And," JB continued. "if I were you, Len Matthews, I wouldn't use your bio and the word honesty in the same breath."

"Why, whatever do you mean, sir?"

"I saw the biography you turned in for the show programs. The South you talk about growing up in has nothing to do with any youth you've ever told me about."

"Moi?"

"Len, you made your childhood sound more like Scarlett O'Hara's than Margaret Mitchell did....and she invented it, with an nudge from David O. Selznick."

JB spotted a stack of catalogs for the current auction. He picked one up and read the cover.

"Is that what you're going on about, JB? So I embellished a tad. It's like a woman adding a scarf to an outfit. It makes it prettier."

"Len, you can't have your entire life be about accessorizing. Although, Lord knows, you do try. It must be exhausting just remembering it all. You know Chanel invented the little black dress for a reason. Sometimes you have to get back to basics, by that I mean the real person you are instead of some made-up persona you think people expect. I'm putting this in dressmaking terms to continue the cutesie metaphor you used, and because I think you'll understand it....and, Len, I really need you to understand. Do you get what I'm getting at, Len?"

He reluctantly nodded his head. "I should stop

playing diva at rehearsals and get along with Dalton, right?"

JB looked to the heavens. "Thank you, Coco."

"I suppose you're right. But Dalton has to take some of the responsibility. He does provoke me."

"Len, the mood you've been in lately the kid who brings in our lunch orders provokes you."

"Oh, he does not. It's not that bad."

"Sweetheart, he asked for a twenty percent raise in his tip as hazardous duty pay."

"And you say I embellish."

"OK. So it was only ten percent. Do you have twenty dollars?"

"Of course I do." He reached into his bag, pulled out his wallet, found the bill and handed it over. "OK. I'll be nicer to the cast and the deli boy. However, I make no promises about Dalton. What do you want twenty for?"

"To buy a catalog for today's auction. It starts in ten minutes. I think I found something. It's not one of the items up for sale, but it's who we've been looking for."

"Maybe you found what you want. But that's not what I came on this cock-a-mamie antique safari for." He grabbed the catalog from JB. "Is there an armoire in this thing?" He flipped the pages.

"I don't know. But we have a few minutes to find out."

They entered the auction rooms. Furniture of all descriptions was placed neatly around the perimeter of the space. Each was tagged with a lot number and each would be sold at the soon-to-begin auction in numerical order.

At the front of the room were several rows of chairs arranged in a half circle. They surrounded a podium with a long table next to it. Maybe ten people milled around the room inspecting the goods on display.

"Well, this doesn't look very promising," Len said. "What did you find in this that was so interesting?" He held up the auction catalog.

"Look at the list of names that are selling today."

The third down read: "Items from the collection's of Harrington Blair Davenport."

"That sounds like a Harry to me. How about you?"

"I'll give you a Harry this time." Len handed the catalog back to JB. "But only because I see a possible armoire over in that corner."

He moved off in the direction of his find. JB went to the last row of seats and began to flip through the pages of the catalog.

Len stopped in front of a medium sized Art Deco bar cabinet, knelt down, and began to inspect the piece. Hovering behind him, like a vulture over carrion, was one of those glasses on a neckchain kind of women. She was obviously resisting the urge to rub her hands together as maybe too over the top. She stepped up beside Len and began to talk at him.

As the two, still in conversation, moved off to another corner of the room the auction began with a matching nineteenth-century walnut bed and dresser as Lot #1.

Len found out the woman at his elbow was the current owner of the auction house—after poor Murray, her late husband, had passed on. While telling Len this she led him to a late nineteen twenties painted Egyptian-style cupboard.

Len decided it was too small but did ask

Mrs. poor Murray a single question about the Davenport collection. She was like a dam bursting, with everything awash and floating with tidbits of information. She filled him in on all the talk about town, not bothering with the facts when a rumor would do.

A moment later she pointed out another younger woman. This woman was standing alone against the wall watching the proceedings. Not unattractive, but not pretty either, she gave meaning to the word blah. She was wearing a cloth coat and tam that had gone out of fashion at least twenty years before. She was identified to Len as the daughter of Mr. Davenport himself.

Len, doing something he'd done since his first days at New York's Academy for Acting Arts, invented a story about the woman from only what he could observe. It was silly, but it was a habit that still hung on from all those years ago.

He saw a woman who had found life much too frightening to handle and so had escaped it by living in a remembered and, presumably more comforting past. She, in order to remain in that past, had done nothing to enhance her person. No makeup or hair styling, nothing that might make one take any notice of her. The most outstanding feature about her was the now retro-style clothing she had on. What a shame, he thought.

Len returned his attention to Mrs. poor Murray as she continued to spew her story.

At Lot #32, an Edwardian salt cellar, JB began to wonder where Len had disappeared too.

Len sat beside him when Lot #34, a Victorian era what-not stand with shelves and turned rope-style legs, came up for bid.

"Where did you get off too?"

"I'll explain later. How's the auction?"

"This has got to be the most eclectic collection of little bits and pieces I've ever seen. Nothing of any great value. Someone just paid forty dollars for a chalkware poodle. That's the most excitement there's been so far."

Len looked around at the sparsely attended proceedings. "Well, no wonder. Eight people don't make for a whole lot of thrills."

"It's more like twelve, but you're right. Mr. Davenport's collection isn't generating much interest."

"Good," Len replied. "That means I can get what I want at a good price."

"What's that?"

"That Deco bar over there."

"Uh....Len, not that its any of my business, but isn't a bar the last thing a recovering alcoholic would need?"

"Don't' be silly. It's not for drinking. Well, it was originally, but not anymore. Now it's a wonderful piece of early thirties Americana. I love the period. It has lots of shelves and it looks nice. It will fit the wall in my apartment like a glove and I'm sick and tired of looking for something that's right. If I get it cheap even better."

Just then Lot #47, a cookie jar in the shape of Walt Disney's *Snow White* came up for sale with an initial bid of three hundred. The auctioneer in minutes had the bid to fifteen hundred, and had it sold to the phone bid for twenty-five hundred in only a few more moments.

"Wow! That went fast. And for so much money. What's a phone bid?"

"You see that bank of people over there?" JB pointed to the table next to the auctioneers podium, which now had six men and women sitting at it. Each had a phone to their ear. "They're speaking with people interested in specific articles in the catalog. When the items come up the auction house people bid for the people on the phone. You may not get the bargain you thought you would."

Len slouched down in his seat.

While they waited for Len's item to be called he skimmed over what he was able to find out from Mrs. poor Murray to JB. Pointing out Davenport's daughter he said, "She isn't much of a much is she? But it's weird, I feel like I know her. Like we have some connection. Maybe I knew her in a past life."

"You're not going to start going all strange and mystic on me and begin channeling some crazy sixty-thousand year old sage, are you?"

"Of course not. Besides, if I was to channel anyone it's going to be Tom Selleck in his underwear."

"Not nude?"

"I still like a little mystery, JB. Anyway, taking them off gives us something to do while we get to know each other. Now, hush, here comes my bar."

"Lot number seventy. A Deco style bar or sideboard. We'll start the bidding at five. Do I hear five hundred?"

Len raised his hand.

The auctioneer pointed at Len. "That's five. Five-fifty? Five-fifty. Who'll give me six?"

Len looked around the room to see who might be bidding against him. Still standing at the side of the room was Davenport's daughter. She caught Len's eye and stared at him, her gaze not wavering an inch. That look captured his attention and they spent moments appraising each other. Len again sensed that feeling of attachment. Why?

The moment between them was broken when she turned away and faced the auctioneer.

"That's seven hundred. Seven hundred. Do I have more?"

JB nudged Len. "If you want the piece you need to raise the bid? It's at seven."

"What? Oh sure....one thousand."

The auctioneer perked up. "I have one thousand. Do I have more? No? Last call. Sold to the gentleman for one thousand." His gavel slapped hard on the podium.

"Congratulations." JB said. "You just spent three hundred dollars more than you needed too. What are you nuts?"

"What? No. One thousand is what it might be worth. Less if it's a copy." Len stopped, looked at JB and said, "I just did what!"

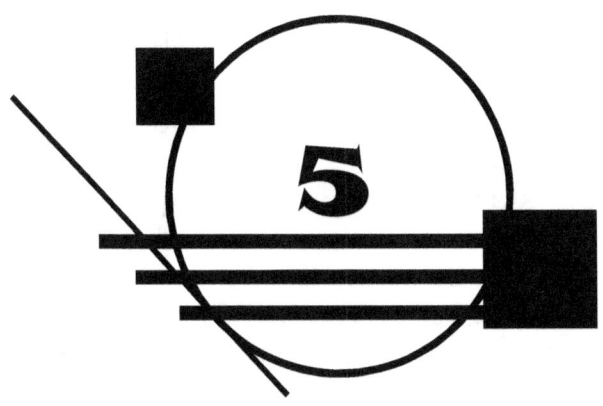

5

oby, JB and Len were back at their apartment building after spending most of their day searching for information that might have led to the mysterious Harry of the answering machine tape.

Toby laid two pieces of paper on the table. One was a listing from the library book on Foundations, the other a listing from the current *Who's Who In America.*

JB eyed the papers in front of him. "So, this is what you were able to find?"

"Right. And I'm pretty sure it's the man we're looking for. His name is...."

"Harrington Blair Davenport!"

JB shook his head. "Len, you couldn't have held that in for a few more moments?"

"I'm sorry, JB. I got excited."

Toby was surprised. "Len, how could you-have known that?"

"I didn't. That's the name of the man we found."

JB faced Toby. "And it's the same name you came up with?" Toby nodded. "Well, if we each got the same person we may have found our possible murder victim."

JB started to read the paper, then lifted his eyebrows in confusion. He handed the paper to Toby. "Can you translate this?"

The listing read: DAVENPORT, HARRINGTON BLAIR, lawyer, philanthropist; b. West Hampton, NY, July 14, 1904, P. George and Gertrude (Wayne) D; m. Lucinda Elizabeth (Royalton), Sept. 16, 1943: child: Brett D; div. 1952; m. Dorothy (Grayheart), Mar. 7, 1952; child: Elizabeth (Lisa), div. 1971: BA, Columbia U 1940, Mlwy, with honors,1944; joined O'Boyle, Grayheart, and Baldwin, 1945, pard. 1951; ret. 1980: Philanthropic. Davenport Found.-est. 1982; Mem. GMHC, GLADD, HRC, NGLTF; Office: 22 Park Avenue South, 10166-0008.

"OK. This is what it all means. Harrington.... or Harry....Davenport was born in 1918. That means he's in his eighties now. His parents were George and Gertrude....She was Gertrude Wayne before. Both parents are deceased. That's not surprising. Harry's in his eighties. In 1947 he married Lucinda Royalton. Who came from a very wealthy family, by the way. I cross-checked it. They had one child....a boy, Brett. Harry and Lucinda were divorced in 1952. Then he married Dorothy....who just happened to be the daughter of one of his law partners....that same year. They had a daughter, Elizabeth, known as Lisa.

He and Dorothy divorced in 1971. Harry retired from the law in 1980. He started the Davenport Foundation in 1982. What's really interesting are his organizational memberships. They're all gay related groups."

"That's easy enough," Len said. "After his divorce from his second wife he came out. At fifty-something, mind you. Once he was out he became involved in the Gay Rights Movement. Quite radical actually. That's why he has the memberships."

"And that would explain the purpose for his Foundation too." Toby handed the second piece of paper to JB.

This listing read: DAVENPORT FOUNDATION: established-1982; purpose: To aid in the establishment of Gay Community Centers in cities or towns that are not currently served by any cohesive community of Gay, Lesbian. Bisexual, or Transgendered factions. Funding grants are awarded each year to groups who qualify. Send for prospectus and qualifications. Offices: 212 Park Avenue South, NYC, 10166-0008.

Len once more piped up. "And, it's the reason behind the auction. The Foundation....which is administrated by Harry's daughter. You know, JB, the little wren girl we saw at the auction house. Anyway, the Foundation, according to rumor, is in dire straits and needs money desperately. Or it won't be able to meet its yearly budget. So, Harrington Davenport is selling off his antiques and collections to save his daughters butt and to keep the Foundation afloat. He...."

"Wait a second here. How have you become Sherlock Holmes all of a sudden?"

"I schmooze people, JB. And the owner of the

auction house was a veritable fountain of information. I told you I spoke to her. Now Toby has found
the basics, the outline if you will. But I was able to
get the deep down, ground in, gritty type dirt. Gos-
sip is such fun when practiced by an expert. And
that lady at the auction house belongs on the Olym-
pic team."

JB said, "And you, I'll bet, would be her coach."

Len glared a few daggers at him. "Do you want
this information or not?"

JB nodded.

"OK, then. Since it cost me a thousand dollars, listen up." Len went on. "Harrington's son....his
name was Brett....was killed by some rough trade he
picked up in the Village in the late seventies. Harry
blamed himself, especially since he was a practicing
homo who was deep in his own closet at the time. He
hadn't been able to really connect with his son. After
the boy was killed he divorced his second wife, came
out, and joined the gay movement. The foundation
is a sort of memorial to the boy. A nice idea, isn't it?
But now, Harry's gotten a lot older and the foundation hasn't been holding up very well. A too generous grant policy is one reason. And there are rumors
surrounding the daughters capabilities too."

JB asked, "Where did the money come from?"

Len went on. "Most of Harry's money came from
his first wife. Then from some very smart investing
he turned it into a whole lot more. The second wife
wasn't any slouch in the money department either,
so he's ended up a very rich old man. Who does what
he damn well pleases it looks like. And, according
to Mrs. poor Murray, he's pleased to cause a major
scandal of late."

"What's that?"

"Oh, get this. He's gone absolutely ga-ga over a twenty-two year old tootsie-slash-gigolo-slash-gold-digger named Tristen. Harry has moved him into the family townhouse and has let him run wild with his money. Society, or at least the circles Harry runs in, are supposed to be....how you say....shocked."

"Wait. Harry's in his eighties and he's taken up with a twenty-two year old?"

"Yep, juicy, isn't it?"

"More like slimy." JB sat back in his chair. "But it looks like you got your money's worth in information. You did well, my friend."

"I don't know. A thousand dollars for a copy of a thirty's bar isn't all that great a price to pay."

"But the information is worth that and more. And who knows? The cabinet could turn out to be worth more than you paid."

"Do you think so?"

"No. Sorry. Actually, I had a chance to look the piece over before we left. Was Thailand a big furniture making center during the thirties?"

Len moaned.

"So," JB said. "Harry has a young tootsie? He would be a good possible as to who'd want to do him in."

"Cher chez la Hommé, as the French queens like to say," Len said.

Toby said, "You've come to a cliched and pretty obvious conclusion haven't you, JB?"

"Well, sometimes obvious is the only possible conclusion. That's why the butler is always a suspect in these things. The tootsie is so young. Twenty-two is what Len said? And Harry's eighty something? That smacks of some major hanky-panky, and its way to suspicious to ignore. What does a kid like that see in such an old man. Other than his money, of course."

Toby gave JB a cold look across the table. "JB, you can't possibly mean what that sounds like. You can't be saying what could someone younger, say twenty-two....or even twenty-six....see in someone older, say eighty-something....or, maybe forty-one," Toby's voice was colored a blue-black. "You're talking pots and kettles here, JB."

"No, Toby. That's not what I mean at all. And I'm only forty and a half." He sighed. "Toby, I'm well aware that there's a difference in our ages, but that gap is nowhere near as wide as these two. It's sixty years between them. What could they possibly see in each other?"

"I think it would probably depend on the eighty-something year old. Right?" There was now a white frost covering his dark tone. "Or the forty-one year old."

"Forty and a half."

Len interjected. "Hold it. If this is going where it seems to be headed, I think I'll just head on out and follow up on a piece of information I just this second thought of." Len stood and went to the door. "So long folks." He waved. "Oh, call me later, JB." He was gone.

THE GREENHOUSE MURDER
ACT I, scene 4

THE LIGHTS COME UP STAGE RIGHT WHERE A TWO LEVEL SCAFFOLD HOLDS THE SET FOR THE SCENE. THE UPPER LEVEL REPRESENTS AN EFFICIENCY APARTMENT. THE AREA BELOW IS DARK.

THE APARTMENT HAS A SINK AND SMALL OVEN WITH BURNERS ON THE BACK WALL. THERE IS AN OPEN MURPHY BED AND A SMALL TABLE AND CHAIRS—NOT GRAND BUT FUNCTIONAL. CURRENTLY OCCUPYING THE APARTMENT ARE GRAY AND A YOUNGER MAN.

THE YOUNG MAN IS IN HIS MID-TWENTIES AND GOOD-LOOKING IN A TOUGH SORT OF WAY. WHAT IS CALLED IN THE VERNACULAR—ROUGH TRADE. HIS NAME IS TOM POLANSKI.

GRAY
(PACING THE SMALL ROOM)
All right, Polanski. You know, with your prior record this doesn't look good for you.

TOM
(SITTING AT THE TABLE)
I didn't do nothing. Besides, if you people would stop hounding me all the time I might be able to go straight. I got me a good caretaker job here—and I pay rent, and....

GRAY
(LEANS OVER TOM. HE IS ON THE ATTACK)
And molest young boys? Then kill them? Is that how you're going straight, Tom? That way will take you straight to Hell.

TOM
No! I don't know what you're sayin'. I didn't hurt nobody.

GRAY
(IN FOR THE KILL)
You're a caretaker, right? You have tools, right? The victim was beaten to death with a hammer, right? Do you have a hammer, Tom?

TOM
Sure I do. But lots of people have hammers. Why are you askin' me? Ask someone who might have a reason for hurtin' somebody. Not me.

THE LIGHTS FADE AND THEN COME UP ON ANOTHER APARTMENT SET AT STAGE LEFT.

IT IS A SMALL SHABBY ROOM SIMILAR TO THE ROOM IN THE LAST SCENE. THERE IS THE SAME PEDESTAL SINK AGAINST THE WALL. A HOT PLATE STANDING ON A SHELF NEXT TO THE SINK. THIS ROOM HAS AN IRON POST BED, A SMALL TABLE BY THE BED. A KITCHEN TABLE WITH TWO CHAIRS STANDS CENTER. CUTOUTS FROM MAGAZINES DECORATE THE WALLS

JOEY HILTON AND ANOTHER MAN ARE
SITTING AT THE KITCHEN TABLE.
THIS MAN IS OLDER, IN HIS FIFTIES, WITH
GRAY HAIR AND A HEAVY MUSTACHE. HIS NAME
IS PAVLOV YURKA.

JOEY
(GENTLY. CONCERNED.)
Mr. Yurka, where were you yesterday morning?
PAVLOV
I spend night at sisters. We have big celebra-
tion. Her son is go away to school. I'm not at home.
JOEY
And the boy who was killed here last night?
PAVLOV
(TRYING TO HELP)
I have seen him. Few times. He is new to neigh-
borhood. He bad boy. Work street. Sells self. How
you say?
JOEY
(SURPRISED)
You mean he was a hustler? A prostitute?
PAVLOV
That it. Here only few times. Hang out with
boys from here. Go to greenhouse to smoke.
JOEY
Do you know who any of his tricks...
(PAVLOV LOOKS CONFUSED)
I mean his customers. Do you know who any of
them might have been? It would help a great deal....

THE LIGHTS FADE STAGE LEFT AND RISE ON
CENTER STAGE.

THIS IS A LIVING ROOM SET WITH A COUCH, A COFFEE TABLE, A PLANT ON A STAND, AND A BIRDCAGE. THE ROOM IS HIGHLY OVER DECORATED AND MUCH TOO FUSSY, WITH DOILIES ON THE COUCH, TOO MANY NICKKNACKS, ETC.

SEATED ON THE COUCH IS GRAY. HE NO LONGER WEARS HIS TRENCHCOAT. HE IS DRESSED IN HIS SUIT WITH A TURTLENECK SWEATER. ON HIS HEAD IS A TURKISH STYLE TURBAN, COMPLETE WITH A JEWEL IN THE CENTER OF HIS FOREHEAD.

SEATED WITH HIM IS A SLIGHTLY OVERWEIGHT WOMAN. SHE IS IN HER LATE THIRTIES WITH BLEACHED OUT FRIZZY HAIR. SHE IS DRESSED AS FUSSILY AS THE REST OF THE ROOM, WITH ROWS OF LACE CASCADING DOWN HER BOSUM, AND LARGE BUNCHES OF FLOWERS SCATTERED ABOUT HER PERSON. HER NAME IS WANDA WHITFIELD.

WANDA
(ALL AFLUTTER, EXCITED, GUSHY)
I can't tell you what an honor it is to meet you, Mr. LaMort. Imagine how impressed my friends will be when I tell them I met the great clairvoyant, Dante LaMort.

GRAY
(FULL OF DIGNIFIED CONCERN)
Dear lady, I have come to you because I sense great turmoil in your life. You must open yourself to the greater power. Unburden your spirit. Tell me of your pain. I know the spirits wish to help you through these troubled times. I am here to channel their wishes for your well being.

WANDA
(IN ECSTASY)
Yes, Dante. How clever you are. My life is such a trial. If only I was understood by these cretins I am surrounded with. Throwing terrible words at me. Calling me dopey and foolish. And even worst things too. It's awful.

GRAY
I see.
(TRYING ANOTHER TACT)
Yes, my dear. It must be difficult having to put up with these terrible souls. The jibes these young people hurl at you must sting deeply. So deeply you might wish to retaliate. To get even with the young boys who taunt you.

WANDA
What? Why the thought never entered my head. No, of course not. I just want them to become believers in the spirit world. As you and I believe. But now that you are here, Dante, I know we can bring them to our side.

GRAY
(STILL PROBING)
But, dear lady, you must carry your belief deep inside against the arrows non-believers hurl at you. That will stop the harm they foist upon you. Do you believe that, dear lady?

WANDA
Yes, oh, yes.
(SUDDENLY ASKING A
SENSIBLE QUESTION)
But what sort of harm are you suggesting? Has someone come to harm?

GRAY
That is a question you must look deep inside

GRAY (cont.)
yourself and discover.
(GETTING TO HIS POINT. HE PUTS
TWO FINGERS ON HIS FOREHEAD)
But I do see a crying and tormented soul. I can
hear its anguish. It seeks the person who harmed it.
The one who forced it to leave this earthly plane and
live in a nether world of darkness and pain.
WANDA
Oh, how exciting. You must tell me who it is. Is
it my Aunt Minerva?
GRAY
(A BIT TIRED OF WANDA'S VAGUENESS)
No, dear lady. This spirit was a victim of bru-
tal violence. A soul who cries for justice. A soul that
wants its murderer punished.
WANDA
Why, that's amazing. We must contact the police
with this information....

THE LIGHTS FADE ON THE CENTER STAGE
AND COME UP ONCE AGAIN STAGE LEFT.
JOEY IS STILL QUESTIONING PAVLOV. BUT IT IS
NO LONGER AN INTERROGATION. THEY TALK AS
IF THEY ARE OLD FRIENDS.

JOEY
So, Pavlov, I'm glad you have an alibi. And its air-
tight. With witnesses. That is if you haven't got your
sister to break the law and lie for you. You haven't
done that have you? I would hate to have to haul
you to the hoosegow for telling a lie, old man. You
wouldn't like jail I don't think.

PAVLOV
(MATTER OF FACT)
Why? I not need her to lie. No reason. I have done
nothing except tell the truth
(HE LEANS IN TOWARD JOEY)
We, in my country, believe that if a murder
has been done and the killer is near a dog will begin
to howl in mourning. And then everywhere the killer
goes dogs will howl at him for the rest of his days. I
don't hear howling. Do you?
JOEY
(GRINS)
Yeah, that might be true where you come
from. Where is that? Poland? In this country we
believe a person is only guilty if it can be prov-
en. So, for now, you're off the hook. But I don't
want you going anywhere without telling me....

THE LIGHTS FADE DOWN ON STAGE LEFT
AND COME UP ON STAGE RIGHT. TOM POLANSKI
AND GRAY (GRAY IS ONCE MORE WEARING HIS
TRENCHCOAT) ARE TOGETHER ON THE STEPS
GOING DOWN TO THE LOWER LEVEL.
THIS ROOM IS A WORKROOM. A BENCH RUNS
AGAINST THE BACK WALL. ABOVE THE BENCH IS
PEGBOARD FILLED WITH VARIOUS TOOLS HANG-
ING ON HOOKS. THE PEGBOARD IS PAINTED DARK
WITH A LIGHTER SPOT BEHIND EACH TOOL HUNG
THERE. THE SPOT WHERE A BALL-PEEN HAMMER
SHOULD HANG IS EMPTY AND GLARING. (Staging
note: This spot should be lit from behind to make it
seem to almost glow, it should be made obvious to
everyone that the hammer is missing from its ususal
spot on the wall.)

GRAY
(STOPS ON THE LAST STEP
AND LOOKS AROUND)
So, this is your workroom. Very neat and orga-
nized aren't you? Every tool in its proper place.
(MOVES TO BENCH)
So why don't you explain to me why there is a
missing tool? And a missing hammer at that.

TOM
(LEANS AGAINST THE STAIR RAIL)
Oh, that. I loaned that hammer to someone.
He ain't brought it back yet. Hey, maybe that's the
guy you should be looking for. I bet he might know
something. Then you can leave me alone

GRAY
Who, Tom? Who did you loan it to?

TOM
Who? To the bohunk next door. You know
the handyman. He's got it.

GRAY
Why would he borrow a hammer, Tom? He's
a handyman. Same as you. He has tools of his own.

TOM
(DEFENSIVE)
How would I know? He asked. I loaned it to him.
He's just a dumb immigrant.

GRAY
Yeah. You might be right.
(POINTEDLY)
You know, Tom, I'll bet that guy is so old country
he still has all those old beliefs that they have over
there. Why, I heard that they even believe that a dog
will howl if a murderer is anywhere around them?
Isn't that crazy, Tom. What an old wives tale, huh,
Tom?

AT THIS MOMENT, SOUNDING AS IF IT'S COMING
FROM SOME DISTANCE AWAY, IS A DOG'S HOWL.
THE HOWL IS EERIE SOUNDING AND ECHOS IN
THE AIR. THE HOWL THEN CRIES OUT A SECOND
TIME. BUT THIS TIME IT IS LOUDER AND CLOSER.
TOM REACTS TO THE SOUND.

                    GRAY
          (A SLIGHT SMILE IN HIS VOICE)
Isn't that just like some foreigner? Holding on to
some old country superstition like that. Here we are.
A modern progressive country and people still believe in ghosts and portents of the evil that men do.
            (HE TURNS TO FACE TOM)
But you're a foreigner too, aren't you, Tom?
You're Polish. Just like the handyman next door. At
least your last name sounds like it's Polish.
                    TOM
No, I'm an American. My folks were Polish but I
was born here.
                    GRAY
Then you're too smart to believe anything that
ridiculous, right? A dog howling just because he can
sense the unspeakable depravity a man has sunk
to.
                    TOM
Sure, how stupid is that? How stupid do you
think I am?

THE DOG'S HOWL IS HEARD AGAIN. LOUD AND
CLEAR. AND VERY CLOSE. TOM REACTS BY LOOK-
ING AROUND A BIT FEARFULLY.

GRAY
What's the matter, Tom? You seem agitated.

THERE IS ANOTHER LOUD HOWL. THE LIGHTS FADE TO BLACK.

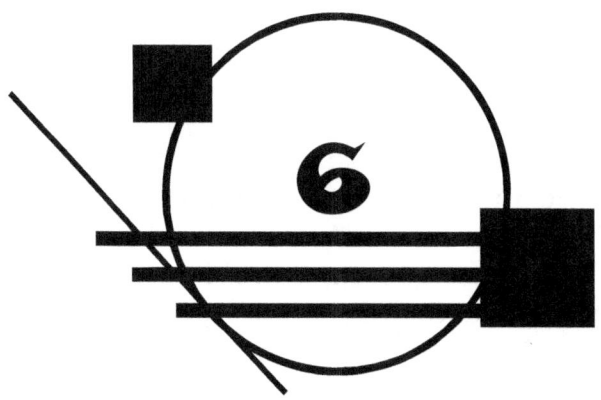

6

The next morning JB knocked on the door of Len's second floor apartment hoping he would join him on his visit to the offices of the Davenport Foundation.

Len didn't answer. "Now where the hell is he?"

JB started down the stairs having every intention of going through the lobby and out the front door. He slowed when he realized that he hadn't said good-bye to Toby. Last nights argument—which JB knew had no real solution unless he could somehow get younger—had left both of them feeling angry. Holding in those feelings led to a lousy nights sleep, at least for JB. Each time he had checked Toby was apparently in a deep slumber.

So a turn at the lobby headed JB toward their

apartment and hopefully a chance to repair this rip in their relationship.

Inside, on the hall table JB found a note from Toby explaining that he had an early rehearsal and wouldn't be back until later that evening. JB knew Toby had to have sat waiting for him to leave so he could get away without having to confront the issue.

JB also realized that one of the bigger problems in he and Toby's union had to be Toby's refusal to deal with problems. Any problems. He seemed to think that if he ignored a problem it would disappear and not cause trouble. So, he refused to talk about anything, which meant that nothing ever got settled. That resulted in the problems sitting there like a huge dead elephant in the middle of the living room. If Toby had his way he would put doilies on the elephant's feet and call it a coffee table.

After locking his apartment JB crossed the lobby again and went out the building's front door. JB could see Len come crawling out of a small yellow tent erected over the manhole in the center of the street. Helping him stand was a member of the telephone crew that had been in the neighborhood for the last week.

"Well, thanks for the info, hon. I'll look forward to your call." Len lightly hugged the man then turned to see JB waving from the sidewalk. He walked over.

"Don't you ever accuse me again of not trying to help you with these investigations you insist on becoming involved with. I just spent a grueling half-hour down in the underbelly of New York City to get information that might help."

"What information?"

"That if your answering machine had picked up

any calls from mixed up or crossed phone lines then they were probably within a five to ten block area of this street. It's unlikely you would pick up Jersey or the Bronx...." Len held up his arms and waved them from side to side. "....or Staten Island to-o-o." He got his expected smile. "So, kemo-sabe, this Davenport person is looking more and more like who we need to find. And, just as an extra tidbit, I am happy to report there are gay people working for New York Bell. Cute ones, too. But the working conditions are abysmal."

"I suppose the sewers of New York wouldn't be four star by most anyone's standards. But what does the fact that the repair people are gay have to do with Davenport?"

"Nothing. But it's helped my love life tremendously. I got asked for a date by that hunky guy."

"You have to be the only person I know who can crawl into a sewer and come back with a date. You are amazing."

Len grinned. "You know, that sewer isn't much worse than some of the bars I used to cruise. In fact it smells better than a couple of them."

"How would you like to go with me to the foundation offices? If this Davenport is our man, he needs to be warned. And soon."

"OK. But shouldn't Toby be in on this too?"

"He's at rehearsal. At least that's what his note said. Why don't you have a rehearsal?"

"I suppose because they're working on a scene that doesn't require me, JB. It's your play. You know what you wrote."

"Not any more. Dalton has come in with some totally new ideas for the material. I sit and watch and don't recognize it as my own words."

"Well, you know my opinion of Dalton Hughes, so I beg you, don't bring him up and spoil what so far is looking like a very nice day. Just where is this foundation located, anyway?"

"On Park Avenue South. Over a couple of blocks and way....and I do mean way....down."

"Then head em' up and move em" out, pilgrim," Len said, doing either a really lousy John Wayne or a very good Barbara Stanwyck.

They walked off together.

The Davenport Foundation had its offices on the sixth floor of a pre-war building in downtown Manhattan. The building's original elevator plodingly carried JB and Len upward. It opened its doors onto a lobby area decorated in what might be called Traditional English meets Andy Warhol.

It had walls of rich walnut wood with heavy white plaster carved moldings that circled at the ceiling. Then abstract paintings and modern lithographs filled the space. Overgrown plants and modern sculptures on dark column stands marched around the edges, with a leather couch or two to break their stride. A thick maroon carpet muffled JB and Len's steps as they walked up to the reception desk.

Behind it was a woman who Gilbert and Sullivan would have called the very model of efficiency. A severe suit on a skinny frame—heavy makeup on a thin face. A nameplate identified her as Ms. Temple.

After she conspicuously ignored both of them for several moments, JB finally spoke up. "Excuse me,

Miss Temple, is it? We'd like to see Mr. Davenport."

She looked up at JB and Len from her chair as if she was somehow looking down upon them. Then using a tone she must have usually reserved for delivery boys and peons, she said, "First, it is Mzzz Temple, not Miss. And, second, do you have an appointment?"

JB put both hands on her desk, leaned in so his face was within inches of hers, and said, "Listen honey....First, I don't care if it's Madam Petrinella Paddyfoot." She stiffened. "And, second, what you need to do is let Mr. Davenport know there are people here who would like to speak with him. It is on a matter of grave importance."

Len leaned over and spoke from the side of his mouth. "Nice touch, JB. Using the word 'grave' like that. Very Hitchcock-ian."

"Len, hush."

The lady, her voice still dripping with sarcasm, said, "As I said previously, do you have an appointment?"

"No, dear, we don't. But the operative word here is 'it's important'. So move your overly manicured brain, do what voodoo you are supposed to do, and ask if he'll see us."

While this scintillating banter was being thrown about a woman was standing behind them, listening to them. At this part of the exchange she stepped forward. "Mr. Davenport is in conference for the day. Might I possibly be of help to you and your friend?"

JB turned to her. She was the woman from yesterday's auction. Davenport's daughter.

She was youngish looking still at thirty-five, and was again wearing clothes hopelessly out of date. Minus the tam she wore the day before, her hair was cropped into a bob and brown—just brown. Her face was triangular with lips that were pulled in tight, causing deep lines to furrow each downturned end. Her eyebrows ran unplucked and uninterrupted across a rather wide forehead. There was also an unfortunate nose. Broad across and short in length, it turned up at the end giving full view to both nostrils, so it seemed almost swinish. It was as if Miss Piggy were an aunt—Porky a cousin once removed. Her eyes were hidden behind large plastic framed tinted glasses so she seemed to be wearing sunglasses inside. Her clothing was an ill-fitting business suit in the wrong shade of green. She had decorated it with a large rhinestone pin holding a droopy pale pink scarf. This woman was in desperate need of a style consultant for an emergency makeover.

"That depends," JB said to her. "Can you help us get in to see Mr. Davenport?"

"Maybe. I'm the director of this foundation. Who are you, please?"

"My name is Jeremy Bent, but call me JB. I have some information that is very important to your father's life." He held out a hand. "And this is my friend, Len Matthews."

Len was staring at the woman. There was the same quizzical expression on his face he'd had the day before. This woman was somehow familiar to him.

The woman said, "I remember both of you. From the auction. Yesterday. My name is Lisa. Lisa Davenport."

Len's eyebrow's rose. This made his expression even more questioning than before.

Lisa continued. "Come into my office, please. Then you might explain what you mean when you say my father's life. That sounds very scary." She turned, opened the door and went inside.

JB walked toward the door. Before Len followed he leaned toward Ms. Temple. "You know, you really have no reason to be so snotty, dearie. You're just a phone operator." He went into Lisa's office.

She was sitting behind her desk. JB sat in one visitor chair on the other side of it. Len took the second chair.

"Now, what is this information you have?" Lisa looked at JB. "You think my father is in some danger?"

Len continued to study the woman as JB explained why they had come to her office. And how a threat of this sort shouldn't be ignored. "Also," JB said, "I have a recording of the conversation. On tape if you need to hear it. Or I have a transcript. I could also turn them over to the police if you wish," JB finished.

"This is all very interesting. A little hard to believe, but quite a story."

"You can think we're crazy if you want, but we heard the tape and we'll both swear your father's life was threatened. The transcript should help convince you of that." He pulled a sheaf of papers from the pocket of his jacket and laid them on her desk.

She considered them a moment. "I didn't say I wouldn't pass on this information to my father. But I see no reason to alert the police about this. I'll take your names and numbers and if he feels he needs to speak with you about this situation we'll contact you. Would that be agreeable to you?"

Len, silent so far, now spoke up. "I've got it. It's the name that's wrong. It wasn't Lisa. It was Elizabeth. I know you. We went to the Academy together, didn't we?"

"I wondered if you had forgotten. How are you Lenfield? Its been a long time."

JB turned to Len. "Lenfield?"

"Yes, JB. That's my given name. But I never use it, so just forget it."

"Not on your life. This is too good to pass up."

Len glared at JB then turned to Lisa. "I saw you yesterday and I knew I knew you. I just couldn't figure out where. You have changed."

"We all do, Lenfield. That was many years ago."

"Not so many. You make it sound like we went to school with Edmund Kean. But what happened to the eager young actress I went to school with?"

"Oh, she found out she couldn't really handle rejection very well. Especially when it came to the eager young actor she married. I married William Taylor. Do you remember him? From our classes at the Academy. We had a child together. A daughter. But William couldn't deal with the responsibilities and he left me. So I gave up my acting ambitions, took my daughter, and came back to my home. It wasn't so many blocks from the Academy, now was it? Just around the corner and into a whole different world, I suppose." She paused for a moment and then sat forward. "And six years ago I became the Managing Director of the foundation. That's when father stepped down. Of course, he's stayed on as Chairman."

"That's what confused me yesterday when you were pointed out to me. The name didn't jibe with the face. I didn't know this Davenport was your father. And he's wealthy too. Is that why you didn't use Davenport as your name back then? So we would think you were poor like the rest of us?"

"Exactly. I didn't tell anyone I had money

because I wanted to fit in. So, I used my mother's name. I also thought it was far more dramatic. Elizabeth Grayheart." She smiled. "It still has a nice ring, doesn't it?"She looked at Len. "But you. What's happening with you now? I followed your career after school. You were doing so well. I always watched your soap, and I saw the play that you were fired from...." She trailed off.

Since the tabloids had chronicled both Len's career rise and his more ignominious downfall with great relish and in excruciating detail her question didn't really need asking.

"It's OK," Len said. "Each of us handles our rejections in different ways, I suppose. But I'm coming back, you know. I'm in a new play. We're in rehearsal now. You must come. I'll get you tickets. As a matter of fact, JB here wrote it."

"That's wonderful."

"Elizabeth, what JB is saying is true. Your father is in some sort of danger. We really do need to speak with him."

She nodded, and then she looked at the watch on her wrist. "Oh dear, I'm not trying to be rude, but I am late for a meeting. I promise I will pass on this information to my father." She picked up the papers JB had given her. "And, Lenfield, I mean Len....please leave your number outside. I hope we can catch up on old times."

"You mean with that bull terrier of a receptionist? We didn't start out very well."

"Oh, she's all right." Lisa stood and went to the door. As she opened it, she said, "As long as we walk her every couple of hours."

She went to the reception desk. "Joan, take these men's phone numbers and keep them for me."

She turned back to JB and Len. "And don't bite their heads off, they're friends." She smiled, made a small wave and went down the hall.

The main auditorium of the theater was under renovation so all rehearsals of *The Greenhouse Murder* were being held in what had been offices on the fourth floor. They were now completely gutted and were simply a large open space with scratched and damaged hardwood floors and a wall of painted shut windows overlooking the lower East Side street the building resided on.

Standing in the center of the space were two folding chairs. They were the only props being used that day. Toby stood next to one of the chairs.

Beside him stood another man. He was Britt Evers, the actor hired to play Tom. Britt was twenty-two. In boxing circles he would have been called a featherweight. He was short in stature, only five feet five inches tall, but broad shoulders and a narrow waist gave an impression that he was sturdy and well build. Flame colored hair combed straight back in waves and cobalt eyes that danced around everything they saw with a smart-ass sort of humor made for an image that somehow forced people to respond to him. That he looked like a magazine model didn't hurt either.

Toby, standing opposite him, looked intently into Britt's face and said his next line. "Well, I trust you today. But, suppose...."

Seated on another chair across from them,

watching their every breath, was Dalton Hughes, the award winning director hired for the play. He concentrated on the two men with an intensity that was so electric people would have been tempted to check his ass for a cord and plug. That he was able to tap into an actors soul and make them act even better than they thought they could was what made him the most sought after director of the current season on Broadway.

He stood quickly and moved over to the actors. He spoke to them almost as fast as he had moved.

"Toby, I need this to be much more intense here. Britt, you've just discovered his treachery. This is where you finally declare yourself. Toby, when he does that, I want to see the panic first, then you realize what he means to you. You grab him and kiss him. With passion."

Toby held up his script. "I'm not sure that's what JB wrote here. I mean...."

"To be frank, I don't give a rat's patootie what JB wrote," Dalton answered back. "This is what I want. Got it?" Dalton went back to his chair and sat.

"Got it." Toby turned to Britt. "Are you ready for this?"

"I'm always ready for making out. Pucker up, my beauty."

"Don't call me that. It makes me very uncomfortable."

"Hey, I call's em' as I see's em'. And you, my beauty, are a beauty."

Dalton interjected. "Can we get on with the scene, please? Now, Toby, I want this kiss to be a discovery. This is where you realize your true self. The person you've been hiding throu...." He stopped. Frozen, as if he was an auto stalled on the expressway.

A moment later when his starter kicked back in, he said, "Where the hell is JB? It just occurred to me that this entire play is about what society has taught men like you. It's about keeping things under wraps. Everything is hidden. It's totally about suppressed desires. And societal strictures. I need to work with that. Where is he when I need him?"

"I could page him, Dalton. Would that help?"

"It certainly would. I just got an amazing idea. A concept that could take this turkey out of the standard genre crap play that it is now and turn it into exciting, fantabulous theater. JB has some major rethinking to do. If he does we could turn this into a smash. Don't just stand there, Toby. Call him."

"That's right, sweetheart.....Well, I'm not sure, but I"ll ask....It would be fun...And we would have a chance to.....What?....." Len was talking on the phone in his apartment. JB was a few feet away making gestures to get his attention. "Just a second....JB wants me." He held down the receiver. "Yes?"

JB held up a palm-sized black box. "My pager went off. I need to use your phone. Please?"

Len went back to his conversation. "Sweetie, I've got to get off....JB needs the phone. But I'll get back to you as soon as I have an answer. All right.... Talk to you then."

Len hung up and made room for JB to get to the instrument. As JB dialed he turned to Len. "Lord, I'm so sorry I ever bought this damn pager. It makes me feel like a slave attached to his master."

"And not a dog collar or studded paddle in sight. Tsk-tsk. But you know what you should do? Set the thing to vibrate and store it in your underwear. You'll have a huge smile on your face every time someone pages you."

"Len, I swear, you are the only person I know who could turn Ma Bell into a sex toy."

His call was answered. "Hello....this is JB.... Oh, hi....OK....Well, as soon as I can....in about thirty minutes?....OK?" He hung up the phone. "That was the theater. Master Dalton seems to have come up with a blindingly original new concept. I have to get there right away."

"And my call was from Lisa. You know it's nice to be talking with her—catching up on old times. It seems like yesterday though. Anyway, Lisa told her father about our visit. He wants to meet us very soon. She asked if we would come for lunch."

"Where? When? And, of course, How?"

"Tomorrow. At their townhouse. JB, it's only a few blocks from here. And guess what, I don't have a call for rehearsal until late tomorrow, so I could go. How about you?"

"And guess what? It sounds like you really want to go." JB chuckled. "OK. I'll be there. At least as far as I know. It depends on what Dalton has come up with. His ideas always seem to mean rewrites and late hours for me. But I'll take the time if I can."

"But, JB, Dalton's won an OBIE for God's sake."

"Len...."

"You know," Len continued. "I'll bet Toby will want to come to this lunch too."

"I'll ask him when I get to the theater." JB looked at his watch. "I've got to get going. I'll see you later."

They hugged and JB left.

THE GREENHOUSE MURDER
ACT II, scene 1

LIGHTS UP ON A COFFEE SHOP. GRAY SITS AT ONE OF THE TABLES WITH JOEY SITTING ACROSS FROM HIM. STANDING BETWEEN THEM IS DOLLY, WHO IS THEIR WAITRESS. SHE HOLDS A PAD IN HER HAND.

TYPICAL OF HER PROFESSION SHE HAS DYED RED FRIZZY HAIR, CHEWS A WAD OF GUM, WEARS A PINK UNIFORM, AND HAS A LARGE FLOWERY HANDKERCHIEF WORN AS A CORSAGE ON HER LEFT SHOULDER.

DOLLY

So, Gray, what'll I get ya?
(SHE LEANS OVER SO SHE CAN
LOOK DIRECTLY INTO GRAY'S EYES.)
As if there's anything I have that I wouldn't give ya for free. When are we gonna go off together, honey?

GRAY

I'll have just a great big beautiful....cup of your best coffee, sweetheart. With cream this time. But one of these days I'm going to ask for that gorgeous hand of yours in marriage.

DOLLY

Ahhh, I don't want to marry ya, sweetie. I just want ta' pleasure ya a little.
(SHE OPENS A BUTTON ON HER UNIFORM AND EXPOSES HER CLEAVAGE. THEN LEANS SO IT IS DIRECTLY IN GRAY'S FACE.)

GRAY
(STARING STRAIGHT AT THE MOUNDS SHE HAS PRESENTED FOR HIS INSPECTION.)

Just talking with you, honey, gives me more pleasure than a grown man can stand.
(HE PULLS HIS EYES FROM HER CLEAVAGE AND LOOKS UP INTO HER FACE.)
Make that extra cream will ya, hon.

DOLLY

Got ya, ya sweet talker.
(SHE TURNS TO FACE JOEY)
And what can I get for you, sweetcheeks.

JOEY

Gosh, I don't know, Dolly. You're way out of my league. I guess I'll have to settle for just black coffee.

DOLLY

Hummm....Honey, if only ya were a couple years older. And I was a few a years younger.
(SHE WALKS OFF)

JOEY
(HE RUNS HIS FINGER INSIDE HIS COLLAR.)

Zowee! She's something ain't she? Say, when are you two going to get together and be a couple? She's crazy about you, you know?

JOEY (cont.)
(HE LEANS HIS CHAIR BACK
ON THE TWO BACK LEGS.)
And you know what I think? I think you're kinda crazy about her too.
GRAY
Sure I am. But it wouldn't work. We're way too different. We don't have the same interests.
(HE HESITATES A MOMENT. HE
LOOKS IN THE DIRECTION DOLLY
WALKED OFF THEN BACK AT JOEY)
But that's not why we're here. We have more important things to talk about. There's been a break on the Greenhouse case. I just got word that Polanski asked his boss for time off from his job. And he's left his old room and moved over to the West Side. His old landlady said he was a nervous wreak and looked pretty haggard when he left.
JOEY
Well, after you making me throw rocks at his landlady's hound dog for ten nights, just so he'd howl. I guess the guy would look bad. He probably hasn't had any sleep in days. I'm sorry for the guy.
GRAY
Since we know damn well he committed this murder I don't feel a bit sorry for him. Hell, I have more pity for the dog. But now that he's on the run we have to turn up the heat on him. Since every other suspect has been eliminated, to my satisfaction at least, you and I have to make this guy confess to the crime or the police won't arrest him. He's smart though. He won't talk just to be bragging to some of his cronies at the local bar. We're gonna have to trick him into talking. Joey, he's never seen you before has he?

JOEY

No. You've asked him all the questions up until now.

GRAY

That's good. What I want you to do is start hanging out over on the West Side. Be in the same places this punk hangs out. I want you to become his best friend. We've got to keep him nervous. And we'll always know where he is with you around.

JOEY

But, Gray. If this guy did murder that boy, why? I don't get it. What was his motive?

GRAY

Motive? That's bunk, kid. I don't care about motive. It's not my concern. My job is simply to bring this Polanski guy in—for justice. Murder is a crime. The worst crime of all. A crime against what makes us civilized. No piece of sleaze should be able to get away with any murder. It goes against the very foundation of who we are as a society. Everybody deserves a chance to succeed or fail in this world. But that kid—that poor murdered boy—will never get his chance. Who knows what he might have contributed to the world? He might have written great books, or composed symphonies, or painted great art. His life ended too early. He didn't deserve to die.

JOEY

Gray, come on. The dead kid—he was a nothing. A hustler, just a low-life prostitute. People don't have much use for his kind. I don't think there was very much he could have contributed to anything.

GRAY

You don't know that, Joey. And it's all the more reason for his death being wrong. He was just a boy. Who knows what would have happened if he had

GRAY (cont.)
lived a few more years. He might have met someone who could have turned his life around. Instead he met someone who took his life. You see, Joey, what's wrong here is the potential that's been lost. It's those unfinished accomplishments that eat at me. Those didn't deserve to be snuffed out. To be viciously bludgeoned out of existence. That rat, Polanski, has to be brought to justice. He must pay....

THE LIGHTS FADE AS DOLLY RETURNS AND SETS DOWN TWO CUPS OF COFFEE ON THE TABLE.

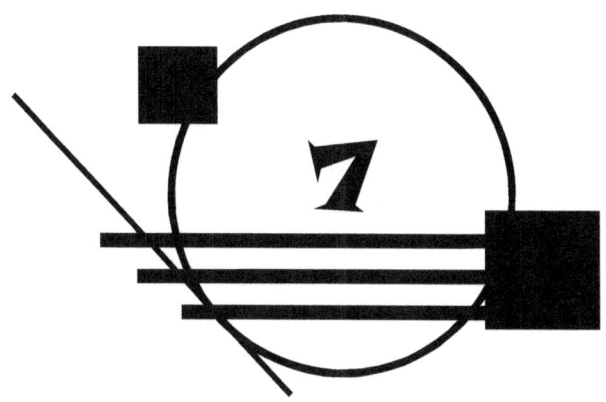

Dalton jumped from his chair. "JB, it's about time you got here. We've got to talk."

He grabbed JB's sleeve and pulled him out of the rehearsal space and into the hall outside. A dumpy flower printed couch slouched against the wall. They sat side by side.

JB shuffled back from him slightly. Dalton's intensity always reminded him of the East River fireworks on July Fourth—all flash and shimmer, and enough excitement to light the world. Leaving behind little puffs of gray smoke to remind you he was there.

Dalton wasn't what most would call handsome. Not with a disappearing hairline combined with dirty blond colored hair surrounding a mostly unremarkable face. His eyes were what grabbed most people. They were a dark pool that seemed to mirror his genius and draw you in like the little girl pulled into the television in the film *Poltergeist*.

"All right, Dalton. I got your page. What is it that couldn't wait for me to be here?"

"What do 'Oh, you kid!' and 'Twenty-three Ski-doo!' mean to you?"

"That maybe you've been hit on the head and possessed by the wandering spirit of Clara Bow?"

"That's it! That's just what I wanted to hear. Not about me being hit....you brute....but that you knew I was using twenties phrases. While I was watching rehearsals today I got this absolutely brilliant idea. An idea that could change the entire known world. That can, my darling, make this charming little murder story you've written a smash hit."

"And what, pray tell, is this idea that you have so modestly come up with?"

"That we scrap all the plans we have for the production so far...."

"Now wait just a frigging minute!"

"No, JB, let me finish. What I'm suggesting is that we change all the plans we currently have . Let's change them to another...."

JB opened his mouth. Dalton held up a finger.

"...era. I think we should place the action of *The Greenhouse Murder* in a whole different time period! Now, isn't that an exciting idea!"

JB waited.

"OK." Dalton took a breath. "So far, we've made this a modern piece, right? And you have to admit that it hasn't been working. Come on. You know it. We have tried and tried and the thing isn't coming together. Now admit it?"

Dalton looked hard at JB. JB hesitated and then lowered his chin in a grudging nod.

"But what if we took it out of today and put it into another time and place?" He paused for a moment. JB didn't speak, so he went on. "What if we placed it in the Nineteen Twenties?" He waited for a reaction. Receiving only a blank stare he started again. "Now what I see is a very stylized....and deliciously decadent....version of the twenties. But definitely that time period. Can't you just see it?" This time not waiting for an answer he went on. "All the sets done in an Art Deco motif, with that wonderful linear décor. And the fringe!" His arms swung back and forth. "Not to mention the colors. It would be fabulous. Very Erte', very Leon Bakst, very Elinor Glynn, very 'It'."

"Well...."

Dalton's own excitement kept him rushing along. "All the characters would wear the clothes of the period. Flapper dresses for the woman and the men in the right kind of suits. With spats. And shiny pointed-toe shoes. And Len! Len could be all in one color throughout the play. His character's name is Gray, so let's put him in grey. A grey suit. You know one of those twenties flannel suits....narrow waisted jacket, with a belt. His body shape would look fabulous in those clothes....and a hat! A grey fedora. It would give the whole play a look that takes it out of the usual mystery crap and gives it a style, a panache, that hasn't been seen around here for ages. What do you think?"

JB waited, dragging out the moment for just a bit. "Actually, I do kind of like the idea. But what's the purpose behind it. The play I wrote wasn't set in any particular time period, but it is basically based on the hard-boiled detectives of more recent vintage. Would the change make sense?"

"Really, JB, sweetheart, of course, we would have it make sense. I have to admit I've been a tad worried about some of the legalities in your little murder plot."

"Not if the plot were placed in say the fifties."

"The fifties have been done to death. But the twenties. For one thing there were fewer laws on the books then. You can get away with more. I've been reading over the script and your dialogue has a ring that cries out for the period. Just a few minor changes and we're there."

"How minor?"

"For instance, the coffeehouse scene could be changed to a speakeasy. We could even put in a Charleston number....just to liven it up a bit."

JB gave him a forbidding look.

"Too much? OK. No dancing. But use a few more of the slang expressions from the period and we've got it."

"You know, it is an interesting idea. I like the possibilities. But I see one major problem with it."

"What?"

"Len."

"How?"

"Well, for one thing, you said he would have to wear a hat. And to be right for the period he would."

"So?"

"Not to state the obvious, but Len is an actor. With the ego that goes with it. And, he is extraordinarily proud of that full head of auburn hair of his. Besides, the press loves it too. There has been more written about that little piece of hair falling on his forehead....no, *tumbling with the grace of a waterfall*....That's what one over-wrought reporter said....than about his acting. It's his trademark. It's been there for years"

"Again, so?"

"So, to be even more correct for the period he will have to slick his hair back. That means you lose the forelock." JB shook his head. "There is no way that you'll make Len give that piece of hair up."

"Humm...." Dalton sat quietly thinking. A moment later he looked up. "I'll bet my next paycheck I can make him change his mind."

"Considering how much we're paying you, I appreciate your confidence."

"But first I need to see the costume person. That is if you really like the idea and want to go with it."

"I do like it, Dalton. But I have serious doubts about Len changing his mind. You're messing around with his image."

"Which it couldn't hurt to change just a teensy bit. If I can get Len to go along with this will you?"

JB nodded.

"Then I guess we have a bet, right?"

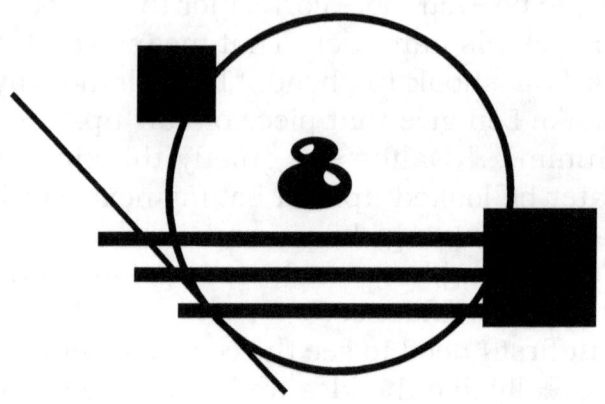

Looking for the townhouse that Lisa Davenport had described to them JB, Toby, and Len found themselves wandering along an upper East Side street dressed curbside with newborn trees housed in square iron fenced plots in front of each of the buildings.

"There. It's that one. Across the street," Len said.

"No. That can't be it," JB answered.

"And why not?"

"Because that's an apartment building not a private home."

"How can you tell?"

"Because by law all apartment dwellings in New York City must have glass front doors. As that building does. It's the fire laws. Only private homes are allowed to have solid wood doors."

"Now who's being Sherlock Holmes? Where did you pick up that piece of information?"

"You schmoose people. I read. I found it in a book."

Toby, who had been walking slightly ahead, turned back. "My God, does he read," he said. "I can't get him to look up most of the time. And forget any sort of conversation. That's totally and completely out of the question. In fact, I'm not supposed to even ask questions."

JB responded in an annoyed tone. "What I'm doing, Toby, is research. It's my job. I'm at work. Would you like me to disturb you while your doing a scene at your next rehearsal? Besides, if you would ask better questions, I might answer."

"I think this is the place." Len had said this mostly from a desire to avoid the incipient argument between JB and Toby than any surety that he had found the right place. That the one he had pointed to turned out to be the right one was pure luck. The three of them went up the front steps. Len rang the doorbell.

It was answered by what in show business is called a stock character. Cast from the same mold as Gale Sonndegard in *Rebecca*, she appraised them and asked who they were in a frigid clipped voice. Strict looking with a pinched face and her hair pulled back in a hard bun she was the type who would scare small children. And at least three grown-ups if truth be told.

However, once sure of their names and seemingly expecting them, she smiled broadly, completely dropping her forbidding persona. Her face, no longer pinched, and speaking with a distinct brogue she radiated a cloying kindness that was almost scarier than what was there previously. Here was one first impression that wasn't in the least accurate.

She obsequiously escorted them in and pointed across the foyer to where Lisa stood waiting in an archway that led to the rest of the house. Lisa took a step down and walked across the foyer's patterned tile floor as the housekeeper lady disappeared somewhere into the woodwork.

"I'm so glad you made it. I hope there wasn't any trouble finding the place?" She hugged Len.

She then shook JB's hand. JB held his hand toward Toby. "Lisa, I want you to meet Toby Gallo. My lover."

She said hello, and then told JB that her father and her daughter were both in the living room and expecting them.

She led the way, taking them down a hallway whose walls were covered in pale silk damask, and hung with gold rococo framed paintings. It was carpeted with an Aubusson runner. At another arch further down the hall she halted.

They looked out on a large living room elegantly furnished with a mixture of furniture from several of the French Louie periods.

Sprawled on the floor in front of one of the delicate couches was a little girl of about ten or eleven, her brown hair in pigtails, playing a child's board game.

Seated above her, leaning his elbows on his knees, was the goal of their days long search. Harrington Blair Davenport.

He was everything, and nothing, like what they might have expected. Knowing he was eighty-two didn't take away one iota from the fact he was still handsome, in the way a Cary Grant or a Sean Connery are beautiful in their old age. White hair waved gently around his head. Still sharp eyes peered from a lined but seemingly contented face. A strong chin gave his face dignity and strength.

Lisa exclaimed, "Susan! You're new dress! And here you are crawling around on the floor."

Susan leapt up, which disturbed the smallish fur ball at her feet. The red-orange ball made a yipping sound at being disturbed then circled and lay back down.

"I'm sorry, Mommy. But Grandpapa wanted to play."

"She's right, dear. It is my fault." Harrington stood up, not quickly but smoothly. "I talked her into a game before lunch. You know how I enjoy playing this silliness. To be honest, I completely forgot we were to have guests. I hope they'll forgive me." He moved gingerly, taking small old man steps across to the group.

They stepped down from the arch into the room while Lisa introduced everyone to her father.

"A pleasure, gentlemen. And this is my granddaughter, Susan."

She now held the bundle of fur in her arms, and just a bit shyly came forward.

A small curtsy and she said, "Hello." She looked at the old man with a pout. "Grandpapa, you forgot to introduce Muggsie." Then she held the dog out toward JB, Len, and Toby. "This is Muggsie."

"Hello, Muggsie...." Len put his hand forward intending to pet the animal. Instead Muggsie bared tiny piranha like teeth and nipped at him.

"Ow!" Len pulled his hand back and put his

finger in his mouth. A second later he pulled it out and looked at the wound left by the animal.

Susan held the dog close to her. "Did the big man hurt my Muggsie?"

"Did I hurt her? That little beast practically took my hand off."

Lisa stepped forward and put her hands on Susan's shoulder. Then she pulled Susan and her pet toward her. Susan's head just touched the top of her mother's stomach.

"The animal is just a little piece of fluff, Len. What damage could she do?"

"I don't know, maybe keep my finger as a chew toy?"

Harrington stepped forward. "Now, now. Muggsie was just protecting her mistress. Are you hurt? I can have Emma get you a bandage."

Len answered. "No, that won't be necessary. But that piece of fluff has the instincts of a pit bull....with none of the charm."

"Why don't we all sit down. I'll have Emma bring in some appetizers before lunch." Lisa went over to the fireplace and pulled on a length of embroidered fabric hanging there. Emma appeared almost instantly. A little too instantly, JB thought.

JB, Len, and Toby all found seats. Harrington remained standing. Lisa gathered Susan to her side so they could sit together in an oversized goldleafed chair facing everyone else.

Susan seemed not to be able to take her eyes off Len. She stared at Len's face with wide searching eyes.

Len asked, "What's up, Susan? Have I got a bird perched on my head?"

She giggled. "No, if there was there'd be bird

poop on your shoulder." Everyone laughed. "But, I was wondering about something."

"What's that, Susan?"

"Is it true that you went to school a long time ago with my Mommy?"

"Well, it wasn't all that long ago. But, sure, your Mom and I went to school together. Why?" Len sat forward in his chair.

Susan looked at her mother. "Gee, Mommy, you were right about him. He does look pretty good for an old guy."

Lisa, embarrassed, said, "I didn't call you old, Len. I don't know where she got that."

Len gave a deprecatory shrug. "I guess to a child her age I must seem pretty decrepit. And, if I went to school with her Mom, I have to be old. Isn't that right, Susan?" She nodded.

"You're forgiven, sweetie. This time. As a matter of fact I guess I am getting old. At least to your generation. But we don't feel it, do we, Lisa?"

"That's right." She smiled, not sure if she should be grateful for Len's forgiveness, or if she should take umbrage at being told she's old. Once again Len's trap had snapped on another victim.

She stood Susan up and while straightening her dress said, "Now, I want you to take Muggsie with you and go and play. We old folks...." She looked over at Len with a smile. "....have some things to talk about. I'll come get you when lunch is ready."

Susan nodded and kissed her mother on the cheek. Then she ran to her grandfather, hugged him and kissed his cheek. Then she went up the step and stopped.

"It was nice meeting you, sirs." She disappeared.

"She is the most delightful child, isn't she, gentlemen?" Harrington bragged.

"Yeah, if you like Heidi crossed with Cruella DeVille," Len said, soto voice, to Toby who was sitting beside him.

Harrington, still looking after the little girl, had a look of doting approval on his face. "Or, am I just an overindulgent grandfather?"

"I'm sure it's a little bit of both, Father."

He chuckled. "I suppose that's so. Well, gentlemen, I understand you have some...."

Just then, from out in the hallway, there came a wail that sounded eerily like a London ambulance heading to an emergency. Then a much too shrill voice shouted, "Get it away!" This was followed by another high-pitched siren yell.

Lisa, walking toward the arch, said, "Oh good God! What's he got himself into now?"

That's when the wailing figure, arms wildly flapping above his head, came barreling down the step and into the room. Running past Lisa he was pursued by Muggsie yipping and snapping at his heels. Together they looked exactly like a mouse chasing a flamingo. Coming quickily up behind the dog was Susan running after her pet.

Still shouting for protection from his micro-pursuer the man circled the room, then leapt up on the sofa cushions between Toby and Len. Muggsie, following, put her front paws on the cushions and continued barking at her prey.

Lisa, evidently used to this sort of disturbance, came over to the couch, picked up the animal, and said, "My God, Tristen. It's just a little dog. It couldn't hurt a fly." Muggsie, twisting in Lisa's arms, kept barking at Tristen.

Tristen squealed at Lisa. "It's not a little dog, it's a beast from Hell. And it's attacked me before. I have bite marks to prove it. My ankles are simply a mess." He lifted one leg to prove his point. "I'll never be able to wear my Joan Crawford ankle strap wedgies again."

The much gossiped about Tristen had made an auspicious, and for him apparently, a demure entrance.

He was dressed in brown raw silk pants, tight and short at the bottom, which showed off his bare ankles. On top he wore a loose blouse in a gold velveteen material. Over it all he had a kimono style robe done in a complimentary Pucci print. A pair of soft evening slippers completed the ensemble. Taken as a whole he looked like a community theater version of *Auntie Mame*. In short, the man was so nelly he squeaked.

"Harry," he whined. "You've got to do something about Susan's pet. It hates me. It simply hates me."

Susan took Muggsie from her mother and held her to her chest soothing her. She glared at Tristen and said, "If you weren't such a doo-doo head she wouldn't chase you."

Tristen, incensed, shouted back. "Who's a doo-doo head? You're the doo-doo head, not me."

Susan yelled back, "Ca-ca face!"

Tristen rejoined with, "Poop-head!"

"Meanie."

"Brat."

Lisa broke it up. "All right, both of you. Stop it this instant. You're both acting like schoolyard bullies. Susan's a child and it's somewhat excusable, but you're supposed to be a grownup Tristen. Shame on both of you. Now, Susan, please take Muggsie with you and go play in your room."

Susan stomped to the arch, then turned back to stick her tongue out at Tristen. Tristen stuck his out at her. She left the room.

Lisa turned back to face Tristen. "Now you're safe, you idiot. Will you please climb down from that silly perch now."

"But it doesn't take care of that little ankle-nipper. And I don't mean the dog."

Harrington sighed. "Tristen, we'll deal with this later. Right now we have guests. Gentlemen, let me introduce you to Tristen Wispe. My....uh-hum.... friend."

Tristen, while climbing down from the back of the couch, appraised the three men. He held out a bent wristed hand toward Toby first. "How do you do?"

Toby mumbled a greeting and touched the extended fingers like he might touch a mackerel. Tristen then held his hand to JB and Len in turn. It was mackerel touches all around.

"So, let me get this right. You're the friend, and you're the lover." He pointed to the correct people. "Then you and I seem to be in the same position," he purred at Toby.

"Oh," Toby answered. "I'm sure there are a couple of positions you can get into that I can't even imagine."

"Yes....I suppose," Tristen replied with narrowed eyes. Just then a muffled ringing sound emanated from somewhere on Tristen's body. He smiled and reached into the folds of his robe. He pulled out a brick sized object that turned out to be a portable phone. He held it to his ear, and spoke.

"See, JB," Len said. "I told you storing your pager in your underwear was a good idea."

Harrington said, "I'm sorry about this. Tristen is a true phone fanatic. If he gets even a few feet away from a telephone he gets the bends." He turned back to Tristen and gave him the same indulgent look he had given his granddaughter.

Tristen lowered the phone. "This is important, Harry. It's Billy. I have to talk to him. But I'll get out of everyone's way. I'll take this to the balcony."

He slid over to a bank of French doors, turned the knob hidden behind the curtains, and was gone. You almost expected a little puff of fairy dust to be left floating in the air.

Harrington moved to a couch and sat. "Now, which one of you has this information I have to hear?"

JB held his hand up. "I guess that would be me." He then explained about the phone line mix-up in his area and how it had recorded the unexpected conversation. And how that conversation represented a real threat being made against Davenport's life, and how it should be taken seriously. JB then continued. "I'm pretty sure Len will agree with me." He looked over at him. "But one of the voices on the tape sounded like Tristen's." Len did agree and nodded. "So, it would look like you have a real problem right here in River City."

Lisa got up from her chair and paced the room. "I don't believe it, father," she said. "We all know what Tristen is like and murder just isn't in his nature. I mean look at him." She pointed toward the windows.

Through the gauze curtains they could see that Tristen had posed himself by perching on the edge of the balcony's iron railing, one leg crossed over the other, and was talking on his phone. His arms waved about with animation and abandon.

Lisa walked over to the French doors and swept back the curtain with her arm. "Now, can you imagine him having the wherewithal to actually murder someone?"

Tristen, noticing the pulled back curtain, wiggled his fingers at the group inside.

"I mean really," Lisa finished. She let the curtain fall back and stayed by the window.

"I have to agree with her, young man." Harrington sat forward on the couch. "It is inconceivable to me that Tristen would try something like this. But, of course, I will want to hear the tape. Do you have it?"

"Actually, I do. But I have a question. Where did you find this boy? Tristen doesn't seem to be the kind of...."

"I know....the kind of person I would have as a partner. But, you have to admit he is handsome. And he is good sex."

Lisa was shocked "Father!"

"Yes, Lisa, even when you're as old as I am there is still some interest."

Len blurted, "Well, thank God, for that!"

Davenport went on. "And, Tristen is amusing. That can sometimes be more than enough. I like it a great deal that he makes me laugh. But, that doesn't answer your question, does it? I met Tristen at a club I belong to. It's called the Minotaur Connection."

"I've heard of that," Len said. "In fact, I have a friend that belongs...."

"Oh, who...."

During this bit of conversation Emma, the housekeeper, had entered the living room carrying a tray that contained a small block of paté, crackers, plates and knives. Just as she bent to set the tray down she let out a loud gasp.

All heads in the room turned to look at her.

Her gasp had happened in response to Lisa, who, from where she was standing looking out the windows, shouted, "No!"

All the heads in the room turned to look at Lisa,

Emma dropped the tray she held. That caused the contents to spill and clatter as they landed.

Now all heads turned back to Emma.

Lisa again yelled, "No!"

Heads turned once again.

Lisa grabbed the curtain, swiveled back into the room, took a few steps toward the group, then dropped to the floor in a faint. Len and JB both moved over to check on Lisa who was now lying on the floor.

Now the rest of the people in the room were split between watching either Lisa or Emma.

Emma had one hand over her mouth and was pointing at the windows, or rather the balcony beyond. Her eyes showed their whites as she tried to stifle a scream.

All their heads turned in the direction she was pointing. Harrington shouted at Emma. "What is it?"

Emma, her voice choked, said, "It's Mr. Tristen, sir. He's fallen! From the balcony!"

JB jumped up from kneeling over Lisa and ran out onto the balcony. At the iron railing he leaned over and looked down.

Tristen, his eyes open and staring, looked up from a lying flat position on top of a white BMW parked in the alleyway below. The car's metal roof had crumpled from the impact and formed a body shaped dent around him. The car's horn was steadily blasting and the alarm system had been tripped. Each sang in harmony a dirge for the now very dead Tristen Wispe.

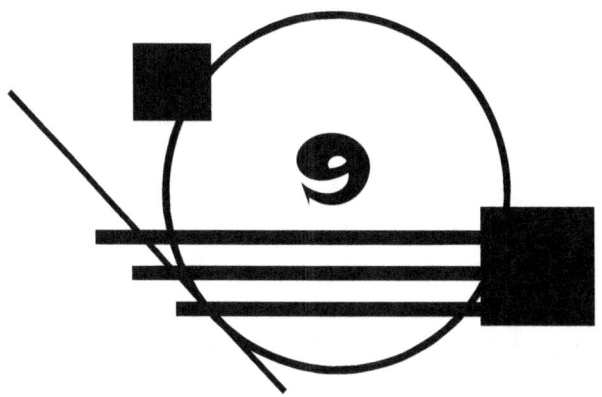

When JB returned to the living room from the balcony he realized that each person there had found some chore to keep them busy. Each was doing something to keep from thinking about the horror of Tristen's fall.

Lisa was sitting with her head back and her eyes closed. Len had crouched beside her and was rubbing her hands and saying soothing words.

Harrington had a glass of water. He was offering it to Emma, and also saying something soothing.

Toby, who had left the room, had, according to Len, gone to call the police.

Harrington looked to JB, there was a question in his eyes. JB answered with a nod. Harrington looked away, sighed, and sat back heavily on the couch. Emma offered both her water and her own soothing words to the old man.

JB moved to where Emma was sitting. "Ma'am, I know you're upset but could you tell us what you saw?"

The lady had no color in her face and little control over the quaver in her voice. She began, but her voice caught on a sob. She stopped, gathered herself, then started again.

"When I heard Miss Lisa shout I looked up. Out there. I saw him....Tristen. He was leaning to far back on the railing. His arms were churning. Trying to gain his balance, I suppose. Then I saw his legs sliding down and out of sight. That's when I pointed...." She stopped. Then buried her face in her hands.

JB turned to Lisa. "And you shouted when you saw him start to fall, right?"

"That's right. It was as Emma described." Her hand went to her mouth. "It was awful." She moved forward. "I have to go to Susan. I don't want her to see this." She stood, but her legs wobbled, so she sat back down.

Len, still crouched beside her, said, "If you'll tell me where her room is I'll go. You need to get yourself a little more together."

"Down the hall, turn left, third door. And, thank you." Len left the room.

Toby returned just after him. "I called the police, JB. They should be here soon."

"Who did you call?"

"Lieutenant Kelly. Who else?"

"Since this isn't a homicide he wouldn't have been my first choice, but any port in a storm, I suppose."

JB turned back to again speak with Emma.

"So you've been Mr. Davenport's housekeeper for how many years?"

Harrington answered for her. "Emma has been running my household for at least twenty years now. And damn well too. She has run the house, looked after everyone, cooked for us, even looked after Susan when Lisa moved back. She couldn't be more helpful." He sounded defensive.

"I understand, sir, and don't mean any offense. I'm certainly not trying to be accusatory. So, Emma, you must know pretty much everything that goes on in the house?"

"Well, I suppose so." She said this as if not exactly sure what JB was after.

"Can you remember anything lately that might have indicated that Tristen could have an accident? I mean could he have fallen before? Or did he have an accident lately? Hit his head or something?"

Feeling now on safer ground Emma said, "He had been complaining about feeling dizzy the last couple of days."

"He said he was dizzy? And no one did anything?"

Lisa spoke up. "It was Tristen after all. He was always sort of dizzy acting, and always complaining about something. We just didn't pay much attention to him after a while."

"The old crying wolf syndrome, huh?"

"What are you getting at, Mr. Bent?"

"Mr. Davenport, a man has fallen from the balcony who we suspect was involved in a plot to kill you. It leaves us with a whole bunch of unanswered questions."

Emma, now totally lost, asked, "What is he talking about, sir? What kind of plot does he mean?"

Her voice had lost the tone of shock and grief from before. She was getting back her authority.

"That's why Len and Toby and I are here today. We have a recording that implicates Tristen in a murder plot. We came to explain it to Mr. Davenport."

"Maybe expose would be a better choice of words," Len said. He stood in the archway. He turned to Lisa. "Can you come to Susan's room now. I think she needs to see you."

"Of course." She stood and walked over to Len, then turned back. "I'll return shortly, Father." Len and Lisa went off down the hall.

"JB, since you've brought the tape why don't we play it for them now?"

"A good idea, Toby. At least we can clear up that part of this."

JB went over to the briefcase he had brought with him. From it he pulled out his answering machine. "The tape will only play on this machine. Is there a plug?"

Harrington indicated one by the desk against the wall. JB plugged the machine in, then waved everyone over. They gathered as he hit the play button. The voice of the now dead Tristen said, "....But he's old. Do we have to kill him"...." The rest of the tape played to the finish and JB turned it off.

"Well?" JB asked.

Harrington nodded. "That sounded like Tristen all right. I can't believe it. He was going to try to kill me." He stumbled slightly as he sat in the chair by the desk.

Emma had been standing next to her employer. "But that second voice, sir. It sounded familiar too. Do you think it was Billy?"

Toby asked, "Billy? Who's Billy?"

Harrington said, "He was Tristen's ex-lover. The

boyfriend he had just before he met me." He turned to look up at Emma. "I'm not sure if that was him or not, Emma. It might have been Billy. I only spoke with him once and that was only so he could ask for Tristen, so I'm not sure I would recognize his voice. But why would they do this? I don't understand." He shook his head.

"They said it on the tape," JB said. "For your inheritance. Money is always a reason for murder."

"But it's so ridiculous. Tristen wasn't even in my will. He stood to inherit nothing."

"Nothing?"

"Mr. Bent, I may be old, but I'm not senile. Or stupid. I was perfectly aware of what Tristen was. There was no way a paid companion such as Tristen was going to get a penny. No one outside of this family stands to inherit anything."

"If I may be so bold, sir?" Harrington nodded, which allowed Emma to speak. "I think the only reason Tristen was here was because he resembled Mr. Brett. Mr. Davenport's son. He passed several years ago."

Harrington took her hand. "You were aware of that, Emma?"

"Yes sir, I was." Shared history can mean that a simple word like family had a broader meaning.

JB was about to ask another question when the chimes from the front door rang. "That must be Kelly," he said. "The police."

Harrington told Emma to answer. She nodded briskly, ran a hand over her hair, straightened her clothing, left the living room and headed for the door.

Harrington asked JB. "Do the police have to know about this little plot. It seems like it doesn't matter now."

"Except, Mr. Davenport, there were two voices on the tape, That means there's another person out there that wants you dead," JB said.

Toby said, "But the plotting was only for what was in his will, JB. And it turns out there wasn't anything after all."

"True enough." JB looked at Harrington. "Maybe we don't have to explain every little detail to the Lieutenant."

Harrington sighed, relief clearly on his face.

THE GREENHOUSE MURDER
ACT II, scene 5

LIGHTS UP ON STAGE LEFT APRON. GRAY AND ANOTHER MAN ARE STANDING TOGETHER. THE MAN IS FORTYISH, PAUNCHY, AND BALDING. HE IS WEARING A BRIGHT PLAID SUIT WITH A MATCHING VEST. BEHIND THEM IS THE BUILDING FAÇADE OF A TWENTIES MOVIE HOUSE. THIS INCLUDES THE CANOPY, BOX OFFICE AND POSTER BOARDS ADVERTISING THE FLICKERS INSIDE. POSTERS FEATURE CHAPLIN, THE KEYSTONE COPS, ETC. THIS IS THE KIND OF MOVIE HOUSE THAT HASN'T QUITE MADE THE TRANSITION FROM NICKELONI-AN TO MOVIE PALACE SO IT IS SORT OF SHODDY AND RUN DOWN.

GRAY HOLDS TWO ROUND TIN FILM CANS, BOTH UNDER ONE ARM. THE TWO MEN ARE IN ANIMATED CONVERSATION

MAN
If I'm going to show your flicker you'll have to pay my price. No pay, then there'll be no play. That'll be ten buckeroos.

GRAY
(REACHING INTO HIS POCKET
WITH HIS FREE HAND.)
All right, I'll pay the extra money. But I think
you're gouging me.
MAN
Hey, I don't want my customers upset.
GRAY
Why should the customers get upset? They'll be
getting an extra film for their nickel. They won't com-
plain, you can bet on that. I just want this shown at
tonight's eight o'clock performance.
(GRAY HANDS OVER THE
TINS TO THE MAN.)
MAN
All right. All right.
(HE BEGINS TO TURN AWAY,
THEN LOOKS BACK.)
Say, what is this film anyway? It ain't dirty, is it?
I don't want my customers complainin'.
GRAY
Nah, it's clean. It's just something special to put
a little pressure on a bad apple that'll be here watch-
ing tonight. So run this before the feature. I want
this beezer to get the point early.

THE LIGHTS GO DOWN ON THE LEFT APRON
AND COME UP ON CENTER STAGE. THE SET NOW
LOOKS LIKE THE INSIDE OF A TYPICAL TWENTIES
MOVIE HOUSE. PEOPLE MILL AROUND AS THEY
TAKE THEIR SEATS FOR THE UPCOMING FEA-
TURE
A WHITE SCRIM, STRETCHED BEHIND ELAB-
ORATE DRAPES AND PLASTER SCONCES, IS THE

MOVIE "SCREEN". IN FRONT OF THE SCREEN ARE ROWS OF RED PLUSH THEATRE SEATS. AS THE LIGHTS COME UP HALF JOEY AND TOM ENTER AND WORK THEIR WAY TO THEIR PLACES.

                    TOM
    Boy, this is great, Joey. I'm sure glad we hooked
up. I think the flickers are grand.
                (THEY SIT)
    I'll tell you what...when we're done ...let's
go to Clancy's. I'll buy the beers. Maybe we can talk
some more about us sharin' a place. OK?
                    JOEY
    Sure, Tom. That would be great.

    THE LIGHTS GO DOWN (Lighting note: The lights need to fade only so the audience will see the actors watching the "movie" in silhouette) SLIDES ARE SHOWN ON THE SCRIM SAYING THE USUAL....LADIES REMOVE YOUR HATS, REMOVE CRYING BABIES, DON'T READ THE TITLES OUTLOUD....WITH ALL THE APPROPRIATE GRAPHICS.
    THE LIGHTS THEN COME UP BEHIND THE SCRIM. A STROB EFFECT CAUSES THE ACTION TO FLICKER AND APPEAR AS A SILENT FILM. THE FILM PERFORMERS ARE DRESSED IN BLACK, WHITE, AND GRAY. THEY WEAR GREY MAKEUP TO SIMULATE THE LOOK OF THE PERIOD. THE ACTION IS ALL IN OVERDONE PANTOMINE.
    THE "PICTURE" BEGINS WITH A WOMAN SITTING IN A CHAIR ENGROSSED IN HER SEWING. THE BACKDROP IS PAINTED TO RESEMBLE A

LIVING ROOM. A DOOR CUT IN THE BACKDROP OPENS AND A CLICHÉ "CROOK" ENTERS. HE IS DRESSED ALL IN BLACK WITH A CAP AND A BANDANNA COVERING THE LOWER PART OF HIS FACE. HE GOES TO HER AND GRABS HER BY THE NECK.

SHE STRUGGLES WITH HIM MIGHTILY, TOPPELING THE CHAIR. WHILE THE CROOK GRAPPLES WITH HER HE TAKES OUT A HAMMER FROM HIS COAT POCKET (Note: This should be an oversized hammer to make it seem more menacing to the audience). HE BEGINS TO BEAT THE WOMAN WITH THE WEAPON. HIS BLOWS ARE BRUTAL AND MANY.

SHE "DIES" IN HIS ARMS.

THE CROOK LETS HER DROP TO THE FLOOR AND LAUGHS A VILLAINOUS SILENT LAUGH. HE THEN GOES OVER TO A PICTURE HANGING ON THE BACKDROP WALL. HE TAKES DOWN THE PICTURE. THAT REVEALS A WALL SAFE. HE BEGINS TO WORK AT THE DIAL OF THE SAFE.

TOM
(REACTING TO THE BLUDGEONING
HAPPENING ON SCREEN)
No. No! NO!
(HE STANDS UP AMD MOVES
QUICKLY ALONG THE ROW)
I can't watch this!
(HE EXITS)
JOEY
(FOLLOWING AFTER TOM)
What? Hey, Tom. What's going on? Are you all right?" What's up, buddy"

THE LIGHTS COME UP ON THE LEFT APRON. OUTSIDE THE THEATRE. GRAY STANDS BE- SIDE THE BOX OFFICE IN THE SHADOW OF THE CANOPY. THE CANOPYS LIGHTS FLASH IN SE- QUENCE LEAVING GRAYS FACE IN DARKNESS, THEN LIGHT, THEN DARK.

TOM, STILL IN A PANIC, RUNS OUT OF THE MOVIE HOUSE. HE PASSES IN FRONT OF GRAY WITHOUT SEEING HIM, AND GOES OFF STAGE.

JOEY FOLLOWS. SPOTTING HIM GRAY COMES OUT FROM UNDER THE CANOPY TO SPEAK WITH HIM. JOEY LOOKS AFTER TOM, THEN TURNS HIS ATTENTION TO WHAT GRAY IS SAYING.

GRAY
That set him off good. It won't take much more.
JOEY
Then you want me to keep after him?
GRAY
You bet. This is just the beginning. OK, Joey, next you have to convince the punk that you're a hood- lum and on the lam. You think you can do that?
JOEY
Sure. But, Gray, I'm beginning to like the mugg. He don't seem like such a bad sort.
GRAY
Don't fall for that. This guy's bad all the way through....

GRAY PUTS HIS ARM OVER JOEY'S SHOUL- DER. THEY CONTINUE TO TALK TOGETHER AS GRAY LEADS JOEY OFF STAGE AND THE LIGHTS FADE TO BLACK.

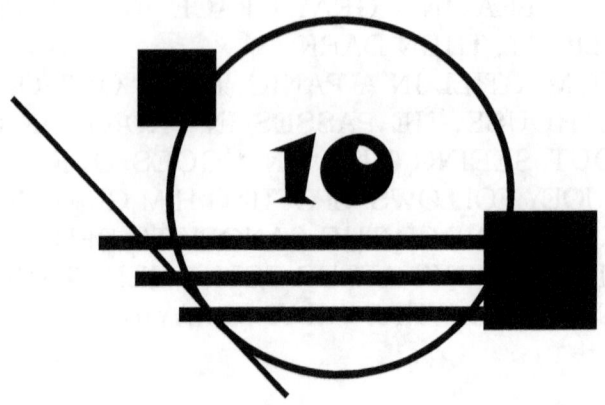

Lisa, on her way to Susan's room, had her back to Len when he called out her name. She stopped at the door and looked back.

"Yes?" she said.

Catching up to her Len said, "Do you want to explain to me what that scene was all about in the living room?"

"Whatever do you mean, Len?" She leaned against the door facing him and was working at looking as innocent as possible.

"Well, I think I understand why you didn't have much success as an actress. You're not very good. At least you're not good enough to fool me. That fainting bit was right out of acting one-o-one at the Academy. That would have been a D minus performance."

As if proving Len right Lisa failed to cover her emotions. They raced one after the other, across her face as she tried to decide what to say next.

"Don't even think you can make me believe that was a real faint, Lisa. It's a waste of both our times."

Lisa sighed. "All right, Len. I won't try to fool you. But I did it for a very good reason. Will you trust me that it was?"

"Of course I will. But why? What was the reason? You're hiding something. What?"

"Please, Len. No questions. I did it because I had to. Isn't that enough?"

She moved close to Len and laid her head on his chest. She moved even nearer. So close he could feel her trembling.

Whether she was trembling from fear or trepidation, or some other emotion, he couldn't be sure. Regardless, Len put his arms around her and pulled her tightly to him. They stood like that for a long time. Long enough for Len to remember a time ages ago. A time when youth ruled and life was only in front of him, a time when all kinds of things were possible.

Lisa looked up at him. Her face was expectant; she seemed to want him to take some further action, as if they were playing a scene from some drugstore romance novel. Len could feel himself almost drawn into her fantasy. His head leaned forward and for one tiny moment he was lost.

A second later Len broke off their embrace and stood with her awkwardly. He had suddenly realized that life had moved on for both of them and some things just weren't going to happen even in the heat of some particular moment.

"I suppose I'll give you a break and I won't ask anymore questions about this," he said. She smiled. He continued, "For now at least. However, we will return to the subject, trust me." Her smile faded. "But, do you think you could answer me a question about something else?"

Lisa made a face of mock annoyance and spoke as if Len were Susan and she was asking the same question a hundred times or more. "What is it?"

"When we were at school you were a spiffy looking young woman. But, really sweetheart, what has happened?" He shook his head. "What's with this retro *Tugboat Annie* look you've got going?" His hands waved up and down in front of her. "It does nothing for you, unless keeping the world from noticing you is your main purpose."

Lisa crossed her arms across her chest. "Don't hold back, Len. Be blunt." She turned away.

"I'm sorry. That was pretty sharp. I didn't mean to hurt you. But even you have to admit it isn't a very attractive look."

"But it's perfect for a single woman foundation director with a young daughter and absolutely no social life."

"Well, of course you have no social life. One relates to the other, dear. It wouldn't be like that if you would do something about it."

"But what?"

"Girl, we happen to live in the shopping capital of the entire world. There are a million stores and a million looks you could cultivate. Everything from street hooker to punk rocker to society dame to Goth goddess. I've got an idea. What have you got planned for tomorrow morning?"

"There's nothing scheduled, why?"

"Because, sweetie, first we're going to have breakfast and then you and I are heading for a fabulous little spot I know. It's called Make-over Island."

Emma came down the hall and stood a few feet away from Lisa and Len.

"Yes, Emma. What is it?"

She took a step toward them. "The policeman, Miss. Lisa. Lieutenant Kelly. He's here and would like to see us all in the living room. I believe he wants statements from us."

Len checked his watch. "OK. But he'll have to hurry. I have a rehearsal to get to. Maybe he can take my statement right away."

The theater stage, since it was freshly sanded and refinished, had allowed the company to move from the upstairs space to the main auditorium. The rest of the theatre was still filled with scaffolds, plaster bits, and paint fumes, all indicating the continued renovations.

The members of the cast were seated in the orchestra section. Dalton was standing on the stage talking through a head set to the light man hidden at his board at the back of the house.

"OK, John. It's better. But make it brighter. I want this to really stand out. Turn it on at my signal."

A noise drew his attention and he walked to the front apron of the stage. "Well, it's about time you got here, gentlemen." His hands went to his hips like a mother scolding. "When I call a rehearsal for a specific time I expect my actors to show up."

"Oh, lighten up, Dalton." Len came down the aisle, up the stairs, and onto the stage. "We got stuck talking with the police. That's why we're late."

"The police? Get picked up for soliciting again?"

"No, dear. You must be mistaking your record with mine. I never had more than an occasional public flirting episode. And that's only a misdemeanor in this state, not a felony."

Everyone laughed. Dalton's smile was only a slight upturn of his lips. He couldn't really show any approval of Len's dagger like put-downs. It might encourage outright verbal rebellion.

He clapped his hands. "All right, children, that's enough small talk." He took command like Rommel in the desert. "Let's get to work." Dalton moved to a chair placed at the center front of the stage, picked up his script, and flipped through it. "Len, we need to work on the second act, scene three, first. Can we have it quiet, please?"

JB and Toby, who arrived with Len, had taken seats at the back of the theater. They were in animated conversation, but lowered their voices at Dalton's request.

"I still don't think we should just forget the threat that Tristen made," JB said. "And, he had a partner."

"But, JB, with Tristen dead the threat has no substance anymore. And the partner, whoever he was, can't do much of anything now. The whole thing is mostly over and done with. And Harrington is safe and sound."

"And who answers all the questions left lying around unanswered? It's just too messy. I like a case to end neater than this."

"So what are you going to do?"

"What was the name of that club that Harrington said he met Tristen at? Maybe we should check it out?"

"It was the Minotaur Connection. But it's private, JB, and open only to cardholders. And you need to be rich to get the card. How would you get in?"

"Didn't Len say he knew somebody who was a member of the thing?"

"Yeah, I think he did. We can ask him."

"But not right this minute. I'm pretty sure that Len and Dalton have something much more important to discuss."

"What? Something to do with the play? If it is shouldn't I be involved too?"

"Not right now, Toby. Later might be a better time." JB settled back in his seat and watched the stage expectantly.

"Can you give that line a touch more enthusiasm, Len? It needs more verve."

"I could....But it wouldn't be the right intention for the scene, Dalton. This section is written dark and moody. And joy-joy-happy-happy isn't right, even with verve."

"Speaking of mood, Len, I've got something to talk over with you. Stay right there."

Dalton got up from his chair.

JB, from the darkness, said, "Here we go....."

Toby stared at him. "What? Where do we go?"

"Just hold on a few minutes, Toby. You'll know everything then."

Dalton moved in next to Len. He threw his arm across Len's shoulder and smiling broadly said, "I've been wanting to ask your opinion about something."

Len, not quite believing Dalton's hail-fellow

well-met manner said with some trepidation, "OK. What?"

"Do you think we have been getting the most that we can from the material as it stands now?"

Len looked out over the empty theater. Since JB was out there somewhere he didn't feel he could say how he actually felt. It could hurt JB's feelings. The real problem was that the play hadn't been jelling. Somewhere along the line in any play's rehearsal life there would come a time when everything began to hold together. When the actors, the director, everybody connected, began to sense the value, the potential, of a piece. That's the "magic" that theater people talk about. It hadn't happened with *The Greenhouse Murder*. Yet. But Len hadn't quiet figured out how he was going to tell JB. And now here was Dalton bringing up the very thing.

"I'm not sure what you're going on about, Dalton. Not to sound too picky here, but I think I need a definition of the word 'most' before I answer."

"What I mean, Len, is do you think the play could benefit from a different perspective? Say, placing it in a different time period?"

Len was still a bit wary. "That would depend on what time period you're thinking about. If you mean Roman times....No, I don't think that would help. Besides I don't have the calves for the costumes to work. With legs like I have I really should be clucking my lines."

Dalton walked a few paces away from Len, then he said, "What I've been mulling over is placing it during the twenties. The nineteen-twenties, I mean."

Len thought a moment. "Well....that's not such a bad idea. I've done twenties style before....in my younger days." He paused for a second, then continued. "In fact, I do like it. Humm, the nineteen-twenties. What does JB say?" Len put his hand to his forehead Hollywood-indian style and looked out into the theater.

JB's voice came from the darkness. "I like it too, Len."

Toby, beside him, turned to stare at him. "You do?"

Dalton had grabbed a stack of drawings from a table conveniently standing at the rear of the stage. The table also held a large square box.

"Would you like to see what we have in mind?"

He dropped the drawings on the stage and spread them out. They were costume sketches of each of the actors, along with a few set drawings.

"They're very nice. But wait...." Len moved the drawings around with his foot. "Where's my character? I don't see anything for Gray"

Dalton had moved back to the table. "Here, Len. I've got them here."

Len went to stand beside him. He took the sketch board Dalton held out, perused it for a moment, and looked up angrily. He shook his head.

"Uh-uh. No way. I know what you're pulling you overbearing twerp. And I won't go for it. I have a contract that prevents exactly this."

He threw the sketch in Dalton's general direction. "That line drawing makes it perfectly clear what you're after. You want me to change my look. Just where in bloody hell...."

"Now, hold on, Len. You need to give this a chance."

"I don't have to give it the sweat off my balls, Bunky."

He took a huge breath, hoping it would calm

him down. Remember what JB said about divas, he thought.

Len went on. "All right, Dalton, I'll give you that it's a passable idea to place the play in the twenties. But let's let the rest of the cast do it. I am not going to go messing with my look." He put his hand to his forehead and grabbed the lock of hair there. "This little piece hanging here has made my fortune. Do you have any idea how much has been written about this hairstyle....this look? I won't change it."

"I have one question." Dalton crossed his arms. "Who does the acting? You? Or that lock of hair?"

Len sputtered. He couldn't find an answer.

Dalton went on. "I know this is new for you, but think about this. How many people really remember you and that look? It was a while ago when all that was news. And you know that theater folk have notoriously short memories. There's a whole new generation out there. Do they remember?"

Len didn't respond. Dalton pressed his advantage. "Now, look at the drawings, please. You'll be dressed all in grey...."

He handed Len a sketch of the suit. The fabric sample indicated it was to be cut from a lightweight medium grey wool. Vested, with cuffed pants, and the coat self-belted, it was the height of fashion for the early twenties.

"Just look at that. The cut is perfect for you. On your body it will look fabulous....and very sexy I might add. And this is the trenchcoat."

He handed over another sketch. It was of an automobile duster in a dark grey herringbone fabric. Double breasted, also belted, with rolled lapels and inverted pleats on the back. It was more than even

Bull-Dog Drummond could have hoped for.

"Then the hair. Center part, plastered down, very Gadsby. No forelock." Dalton held up his hands. "But you shouldn't panic, Len, because there's this."

He snapped his fingers and a pre-arranged spotlight went on. The light illuminated the pink striped square box sitting at the center of the table. Dalton fiddled with the latch a moment, then stood away. Without further help the top of the box sprung up, the sides fell open and presented, minus any trumpets blaring, a man's hat lying on a bed of black velvet.

Not just any hat, mind you, but a softly glowing dove grey fedora. It had a plain tapered snap-brim, narrower in front tapering to a wider side, and was slightly rolled. A five-and-five-sixteenth inch tapered crown flaunted a two-inch band of blood-red grosgrain ribbon with a flat bow along the side.

The hat sparkled in the spotlight with both elegance and panache, with just a little insouciance to give it some kick.

Beside it, stuck into the velvet, was a stickpin. It was made of a bright silver metal frame holding a large emerald cut red stone. Both the hat and the pin were designed to evoke the spirit of the "Jazz Age", of the Roaring Twenties.

Dalton continued his sales pitch. "The hat band and the pin are the only real color you would wear. Everything else is shades of grey. Can't you just picture it?" He said this in exactly the same tone the snake had used in Eden.

"Oh, my God." There was pure unpretentious awe in Len's voice. "That hat! It's stunning!" He reached forward but stopped. He looked at Dalton. "May I?"

"Of course."

Dalton smiled and put his hands behind his back. He did a quick turn and looked out toward JB. He mouthed the words, "You owe me."

Dalton turned back to Len. "Just think what the critics will say if you do this, Len. Wouldn't you rather they respect and critique your acting instead of a lock of hair?"

JB and Toby, along with the rest of the cast, had all moved up onto the stage. They were all anxious to see what this change would bring to the play and their parts. They crowded around the sketches. Ooo's and appropriate Ah's were heard all round.

Len, meanwhile, had moved over to a mirror and placed the fedora on his head. He looked sideways to check out the effect.

While still checking his image in the mirror he said, "Dalton, you are one manipulative son-of-a-bitch. And don't think I wasn't aware of what you were doing. I haven't said I'll go along with this cock-a-mamie idea. But I'll think about it." He adjusted the hat for a better angle. "Lord, this really is one beautiful hat."

JB slid up next to Dalton. "I don't think I'll pay off our bet just yet. OK?"

The show's cast and staff were seated in the first two rows of the orchestra. Dalton sat on the stage center apron giving notes. "So we've got some exciting changes coming up...." He stopped and looked over at Len who was slumped down in his seat. "....contingent upon our star, of course. So, that's it for notes." He clapped his hands. "Everyone who's on call for tomorrow, we start at twelve noon, not twelve-thirty. Good work, all of you."

Everyone moved from their various positions and mumbled and mingled in preparation for leaving. JB and Len found each other and began to gather their belongings.

Toby walked over to them. "Boy, the twenties idea is great, isn't it? Just what the show needs. Everyone is excited about it."

Len looked pained. That's the jelling he had reffered too, and everyone did seem excited by the idea.

JB, who was picking up empty cups along the seats, said, "Don't count chickens that are still in the egg, my love. Len has to approve any major changes in the show he signed for. That's in his contract. But why would he want to hurt the show?" JB looked directly at Len. "Huh?"

Len became busy checking the seats around him, ostensibly looking for his coat.

From across several rows of seats, Britt Evers, the actor playing Tom, called out, "Hey, Toby." He moved sideways through the aisle, which brought him closer to where the three were standing. He smiled. "The gang is going to Joe Allen's. Want to come? Nell is singing."

Toby looked over at JB.

JB said. "Do you want to go?"

Toby hesitated a second, then said, "Yes."

"So go already." JB waved his hands.

Toby got his jacket. "JB. Len. Do you want to come?"

"Good Lord, no," JB answered. "All I want to do is rest. Besides, I have major re-writes to do."

"I agree with JB. I'm pooped," Len said.

Toby quickly kissed JB on the cheek and went

to join the others.

"Nice of you to let the youngster go out. Especially on a school night."

"Cut it out, Len. He deserves to have a life. He spends way too much time hanging around with us old fogies already."

"Watch who you include in that fogie reference there."

"Len, give it up. You're floating somewhere around your forties just like I am. Toby is a kid. A whole other generation. Which, in a round about way, brings me back to my earlier question. Why would you want to hurt the show? Just because of a so-called 'look'? Dalton's right, it was years ago when all that was written about you. Or is this about something else. Like your vanity?"

"Hey! This is your script, JB. It's supposed to be your vision. Is this what you had in mind when you wrote it? Your contract has the same clause as mine, you know?" Len was having trouble getting his coat on right. The left sleeve had apparently vanished. "You said yourself that you don't recognize the thing anymore. What happens after this change?"

"Actually, Len, I don't have a problem with the idea. In fact, I think it will help a great deal." He paused a moment. "Len, you know theater is a collaborative effort. Any suggestion from the team that helps make the show come alive is worth working with. Right?"

Len was standing with his coat on, but looking as if the coat had actually won the battle. "Why do I feel like I'm being picked on here? It's a major change, JB. Huge. Do you have any idea what I have invested in this look? Just in mousse alone. I don't think I'm capable of making this kind of change. It's just too big."

"Sweetheart, for the last year you've been making a change that takes more courage than most men need in a lifetime. You've stayed sober for most of a year. That's absolutely great. So now it's time to grow a bit. That's partly what the AA program is about, right?"

"I don't know, JB."

"Well, do as you promised. Give the idea some time to sink in. At least consider it."

"All right, I can do that. Now get your stuff. We need to get out of here."

Looking around JB realized the lights were off. They walked up the aisle to the still brightly-lit lobby.

"Oh, Len. I know what it was I wanted to ask you about. Did you say you knew about the Minotaur Connection?"

"Yeah, why?"

"Well, that's where Harrington met Tristen, and we know Tristen had a partner in his little murder for profit scheme. I'll wager the partner is one of the members of that club."

"Will you buy me dinner if I tell you what I know?"

"Sure. As long as you tell me things that will help."

"Whatever do you mean?"

"Len, for a free meal you'd tell me the Gettysburg Address in Pig Latin."

"Or-fay or-sca...."

Joe Allens is to Broadway what *Cheers* was supposed to be to that block in Boston it sat on. But at Joe Allen's everybody knew your name because it had been splashed all over *The New York Times* Entertainment Section in reviews and articles when your latest show opened.

Joe Allens was Broadway's neighborhood after-work bar. Of course, after work didn't begin until after eleven PM when show curtains had come down and makeup had been removed. Then the club was filled with actors, gypsies, producers, directors, curtain pullers. All manner of show biz types.

From the entrance the crowded bar ran along the right wall, while booths ran up another wall at the center. To the left was the restaurant with tables at the back and a baby grand piano standing proudly at the front. Stools surrounded the piano and on any given night a player from a current musical was usually coaxed into singing a few songs.

Britt and Toby were sitting at a large table alone, the rest of the Greenhouse cast had moved to the front to hear the singer for that night.

Toby, while he lifted Britt's hand from his thigh, said, "I don't think you fully understand what my situation is, Britt."

"Oh, I understand completely. You live with a man who's old enough to be your father. Not that he isn't good-looking in a renovated *This Old House* sort of way. And you're together in what I am sure you think of as a relationship."

"What JB and I have is exactly that. A relationship."

"And how exciting can that be, Toby? I mean once the guy has his warm milk—at what, ten at night?—isn't the evening mostly over? Whaa-hoo."

Toby started to respond but Britt interrupted. His voice had dropped to become a seductive growl. Then his hand once more slid to Toby's thigh. "When was the last time you felt a hard, toned, muscled chest? Or a bicep that bulges when you touch it, a stomach that ripples as you count the ridges of a six-pac, a cock that pulsates with lust lying hard in your hand, a mouth that envelops you, an ass...."

"Britt, stop it." Toby reached down and covered Britt's roving and squeezing fingers with his own hand. "JB and I have a very special...."

"What you have, my beauty, is a settled, boring, old coot of a partner who probably doesn't have the slightest idea of what fires burn inside you. How your body desperately needs someone to match the heat you give off."

Toby looked at Britt. Amusement lightened his voice. "You've got to be kidding? Where do you get your dialogue? The latest issue of *Stroke* magazine?"

Britt took a sip of his drink. "Well, it must be doing something, Beauty. You've got a hard-on. And an impressive one at that. We shouldn't let it go to waste."

"There's no 'we', Britt. Now put your libido and your hands back where they belong, and you and I will go listen to the music."

"OK, Beauty, but when you get tired of living with your maiden aunt, give me a call."

"Don't sit up nights waiting." Toby stood up and made his way to the piano.

Britt, still at the table, wrote his number on a napkin and stuffed it into Toby's jacket pocket.

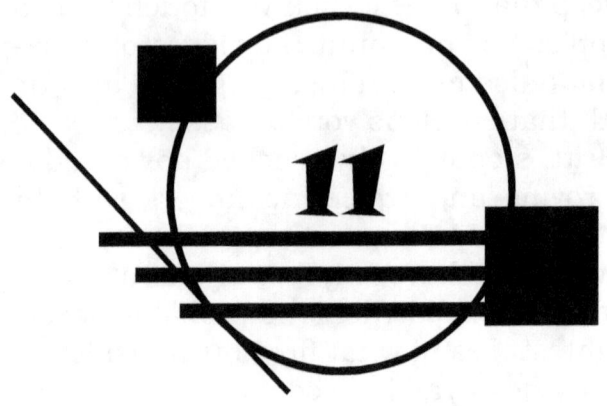

11

New York Police Lieutenant Kelly, after reading the report he had found on his desk that morning, thought about the contents for several minutes, then reached for the telephone and dialed the number he had looked up on his Rolodex.

There was something that didn't ring right about the report. Something that just didn't fit with the story he had been told by the Davenports the day before.

He waited while the phone rang.

When it was picked up he said, "Bent? Sorry to call so early, but I have a favor to ask. Could you come to my office sometime today? I have something of a mystery, and you might be able to clear it up....It would help....Yes....Good....

Then you'll show up here around eleven?"

He put the phone back in its cradle and began to re-read the report he held in his hand.

Within a minute or two of JB's phone call, Len came out of his apartment and went down the one flight of stairs to the lobby. He made a turn toward JB's apartment.

Len was never an up-and-at-em' early kind of guy, but since getting sober he found himself awake at practically dawn. It was a good thing that Lisa was also an early riser since they had a breakfast date.

At JB's door he knocked and waited. When JB answered he said, "Sorry to bother you so early...."

JB rubbed at his eyes. "That's all right. You're not the first today."

"....but I've got a date in thirty minutes." He handed JB a piece of paper. "Anyhoo, here's the number of that guy I said I would give you. I called him. His butler will pass on the message. He'll be expecting to hear from you sometime today."

Len started to walk away, then turned back. "But let me warn you. The guy is a total flake, but really quite nice when you get past it. When you have as much money as he does you're allowed to be an idiot. It's considered charming."

"All right. Thanks, Len. I'll call right away. Since I've got to see someone this morning maybe we can have lunch."

Len said, "In public?"

JB nodded.

Len made a small shrug. "What a good idea. Listen, luv, I have to go. I'll see you later."

JB shut the door and headed for the bathroom to begin his morning routine. But first he sneaked quietly into the bedroom to gather his clothes. He was being extra quiet because he didn't want to wake up Toby.

JB wasn't sure when Toby had got in the night before. All he was sure of was that Toby lay beside him, asleep, that morning when the phone rang. He must have had a good time, JB thought, he hadn't stirred at any of the morning's noise.

Lieutenant Kelly looked up from his desk at the sound of his office door opening.

"Bent," he said. "Glad you could get here."

Kelly didn't change much from visit to visit. He still had the over-the-hill football player's build. The same starting-to-go-grey buzz cut hair and the same dour outlook on life in general.

"Good to see you, Kelly." JB put a cup of coffee on the desk. "I thought this might help. I know the brew here stinks."

The drink was a peace offering in case Kelly wanted to bawl him out for being at the Davenport's when he had arrived the day before. Kelly had a way of making you feel guilty for being in a place that he didn't think you belonged. It was his strongest asset as a cop, the guilt thing.

JB sat in the chair on the other side of Kelly's desk.

"Now, what's this mystery you were talking about this morning?"

"I've always liked that you skip the small talk and get right to the point, Bent."

"Only because I have a lunch to get to."

"In that case, here." Kelly handed over a file folder. "Take a look at that and tell me if you see anything unusual." He picked up the cup that JB had delivered.

JB opened the folder holding a coroner's report on Tristen Wispe.

"Wow, you got this awfully quick, Kelly." JB flipped through the pages in the folder. "Humm.... there's even a toxicology report. It must be dead down in the morgue these days." He looked up. "Sorry. I couldn't resist."

Kelly said, "That's only a cursory check of the body and rudimentary bloodwork. The regular autopsy will have to be done later. But when you have someone as prominent as Harrington Davenport involved in a crime things do tend to get expedited."

"Crime? I thought it was being considered an accident."

"That's part of the mystery I called you about." Kelly pointed at the folder in JB's hands. "Just read the report, and tell me what you think."

JB rifled through a set of photos showing Tristen. He was nude and lying on the slab downstairs. He began to understand what Harrington had meant when he said Tristen was good sex. The boy was definitely well put together, and well endowed too. He stopped at one photo.

"What's this?"

Kelly looked at the photo JB held up.

"That is a picture of the victims legs.

Specifically, look at the bite marks on both his ankles. The Davenport's told us the little girl's dog hated the victim. And those marks are both old and new. That Muggsie sure made a mess of his legs."

"I would say so. Look at that. To the point of an open wound on his right ankle."

"That's what we think caused the victim to fall. While he was perched on the railing the little ball of fluff bit him. That startled him, and he fell to his death."

"Well, the beast does have sharp little teeth. Just ask Len." He looked again. "And that's some wound." JB looked at the photo for a third time. It wasn't right. There was a question lurking in one of the dark corners of his mind. The problem was he couldn't get it to come out from its hiding place.

Kelly, sounding impatient, said, "But that's not what I wanted you to see. Take a look at the blood-work report."

JB set the photo down and picked up the single sheet of paper. "What is it, Kelly?" He read. "Wait a minute That doesn't make sense."

"Ah, you found it. The drug toxicity level is way up there, isn't it? And look at the type of drug. No one mentioned he had any problem."

The report said that Tristen had an exceedingly high dosage level of Labetalol, a beta-blocker that was usually prescribed for high blood pressure. Tristen's level far exceeded a normal dosage for anyone, young or old, with even acute hypertension.

"Considering that he was only twenty-two it's doubtful that he did have a problem. Although I have heard of younger people having hypertension before. It isn't unheard of."

"Was he an addict then? A real garbage

head drug user will take anything if he thinks he'll get a high off it."

"You know, Kelly, I don't know. I only met the man for a few moments. Once. And that wasn't long enough to find out much about him. Other than the fact he was as nelly as a goose in May, I know nothing."

"And the clothes on the body already told us that. I guess I'll have to talk to the Davenport's again. A lot of help you were."

"Hey, I try, Kelly. You just need to get easier questions."

Len and Lisa were standing side by side.

"Lisa, look down there. It's a shopper's Land of Oz. Laurent, Lauren. Armani. Oh, my. Just the names make me tingle."

They were on the corner of 35th and Madison Avenue looking toward the seventies.

"Shop after shop. Boutique after boutique. And each one just waiting to make you beautiful."

"And each one more outrageously expensive than the next. Len, I'm not so sure this is a good idea."

"Lisa, don't pull that *Poor Pitiful Pearl* bit with me. What do you make as the director of your father's foundation?"

"Not as much as you seem to think. I'm just an employee of the foundation. Of course, I'm in father's will....but that won't be until he dies. And then it won't be very much. Most of his money will go to the foundation, I'm sure."

"Well, I would hazard a guess that your idea of 'much' and 'most' is completely different than mine. And it's still no excuse for this *Gidgit Goes Frumpy* look you've got going."

Lisa was once again dressed all wrong. She had on a too long plaid wool skirt, a pink pin-striped cotton blouse, sensible loafers, a print scarf over her hair, and a tan three-quarter-length car coat.

"It might have been fine when we were students but now it looks like you're trying to hold on to something that slipped away a long time ago...." Len stopped talking, and realized what he had just said.

"Len, are you all right?"

"What? Oh. Yeah, I'm fine. But if you see a petard anywhere around it'll have my name on it. I'll be ready for hoisting in a moment." Lisa looked at him questioningly. "It's nothing, sweetie."

Len began to aim Lisa to the first store on their left. "Besides, if we don't find what we're looking for here, there's always the wilds of the West Side. Betsy Johnson, Charivari....Yummm."

That afternoon Len was just turning from the mailboxes in the lobby of his building when JB walked in.

"Well if it isn't Sister Mary Makeover. How's your reformation project going?" JB said.

"Lisa's at the salon. Sitting under a dryer with foil sticking out all over her head. Jose is doing wonders. Together with the clothes we bought she is going to look fab-boo."

"Should I bring up ears and purses? Not to mention sows and silk. What a lot of work."

"You're right. All the fussing can be exhausting. But worth it I think. In fact, you'll see the results at rehearsal tonight. We're going out after to show her off. Tonight is still just a short meeting, right?"

"Right. Dalton wants the producers to see the sets and costume sketches for the twenties look. That is if we're going to do it " JB gave Len a look.

"We'll see. I'm still thinking about it. Oh, how was your lunch? Did you get what you wanted?"

"Yes, as a matter of fact. He was nice enough to loan me his Minotaur membership card. And, it turns out, there's a meeting tonight. I'm going to take Toby with me. He's young enough, so I'll fit in with them. By the way, I may never speak to you again."

"Whatever for?" Len was all innocence.

"That friend of yours. He has to be the biggest jackass I've come in contact with in ages. You didn't mention that he was a total space cadet." JB's hand whooshed above his head. "I mean, like a lap dancer with a dollar tip. Completely gone. And that laugh. You should have warned me about that, you fink. After he brayed a couple of times there wasn't an eye in the entire restaurant that wasn't on us. Quell embarrass-mont."

"Consider it payback for leaving me alone to face those Philistines at Sothebys. Now we're even. And, yes, I love you too." Len leaned forward and bussed JB on the cheek. "I have to get back to the salon. I'll see you at the theater. Be prepared for magic."

Before JB could answer Len waved and was gone.

THE GREENHOUSE MURDER
ACT III, scene 2

THE LIGHTS COME UP ON A PARK SET. AN IRON BENCH STANDS CENTER STAGE. A PATH LEADS FROM UPSTAGE LEFT, DOWN IN FRONT OF THE BENCH, AND OFF STAGE RIGHT.

    IT IS EVENING SO THE PARK HAS AN OMINOUS DARK AND SHADOWY FEELING. ALONG THE PATH WALK JOEY AND TOM. THEY ARE ENGAGED IN CONVERSATION. WHEN THEY ARRIVE AT THE BENCH THEY SIT.

JOEY
(TRYING TO SEEM COMPLETELY
ERNEST AND TRUTHFUL)

Tom, I have to give you the truth. I have a past. And its not pretty. You may not want to keep hanging with me after you know.

TOM

It can't be all that bad. Hell, I ain't no choirboy myself.

JOEY

Can anything you've done get you killed? I'm on the lam, Tom. There's people after me.

TOM

What people? Whatta ya mean?

JOEY

I was in the Dopey Benny gang over on the East Side. They called me Joey Swank. But someone found out I was skimming from the numbers. The rat was going to squeal on me. So I took care of him, you know? What I didn't know was the guy was Dopey's best friend from when they were kids. So now Dopey's out to get me. That's why I carry this.

(JOEY OPENS HIS COAT TO SHOW
A GUN IN A LEATHER HOLSTER)

TOM

Joey, are ya nuts? Ya can get arrested for carryin' that.

JOEY

I can get dead if I don't. I got to protect myself, kiddo. Anyone comes too close I nail them. But now I got to get out of town. Soon. You've heard about Dopey? He's crazy. And he won't stop looking for me.

TOM

But where will ya go?

JOEY

I was thinking California. It's far enough away I can start over. Nobody will know me there. I got Dopey's money hidden where only I know. I was thinking I could try my luck in the flickers. The ladies seem to think I'm the berries.

TOM

(HE THINKS SILENTLY FOR A MOMENT.
THEN HE SITS STRAIGHT AND TURNS
TO FACE JOEY)

Take me with ya, Joey.

(JOEY REACTS IN THE NEGATIVE)

TOM (cont.)

Why not?

JOEY

Because you might get killed. And....I like you, kiddo. I don't want you killed because of me.

TOM

I'm willin' to take the chance. Hey, we get along all right, don't we?

(JOEY NODS)

Then I don't see no problem. Joey, I like you too, that's why I want to be with you....

(HE STOPS. PERHAPS HE'S GIVEN AWAY TOO MUCH. HE BEGINS AGAIN.)

Hell, I could use a partner. I bet we'd do all right, you and me, out in California. Come on....

GRAY ENTERS UPSTAGE LEFT. HE COMES DOWN THE PATH AND STOPS A FEW FEET FROM WHERE THE TWO MEN ARE TALKING.

GRAY

I knew that if I looked hard enough I'd find you, Polanski. You think a move over to the West Side would throw me off the track? You left a trail of land-ladies who didn't like you, Polanski. They all talked to me.

JOEY
(TO TOM)

What's this all about?

GRAY

Didn't he tell you? He's the prime suspect in a young kid's murder. You should stay away from him, Mister. He's a bad one.

TOM

Hey, the cops just questioned me. That's all. I was let go.

GRAY

For now, Polanski....but you and I both know you did it. I just got to find a way to link you to that hammer we found next to the kid's body.

(HE TURNS TO JOEY)

That's right, Mister. This guy beat a helpless kid to death with a ball-peen hammer. Then threw the dead body and the bloody hammer he used to do it with into a ravine. Real nice, huh? You've hooked up with a real winner.

JOEY

He said the cops let him go. So should you. Who-ever you are?

GRAY

(AS GRAY SPEAKS HE MOVES CLOSER
AND CLOSER TO TOM, UNTIL HE IS
FACE TO FACE WITH HIM. EACH WORD
OF GRAY'S IS A THREAT.)

I'm this guy's worst nightmare. I'm the dog howl-ing at his heels. I'm the guy that's gonna prove he beat a poor boy's head in, and then tried to blame a poor immigrant for his crime....I'm the guy that takes the case for a kid who can't fight back anymore. I'm the guy that knows that boy's death was wrong.... and I know the scum that did it has to be punished! You want to know who I am. I'm vengeance! And I'm after you, Polanski.

JOEY

Hey, back away from my friend. You got no right to....

GRAY

Wait a second. I know who you are. It just took

GRAY (cont.)

me a while to recognize you. You're that punk, Joey Swank, from the East Side. Come down in the world haven't you, Joey. Hell you're worst than he is. There's nothin' lower than a thief that steals from his fellow thieves. You shoulda' been long gone by now. Dopey and his boys are still lookin' for ya. So stay out of this, Swank. Or I'll turn ya over to Dopey.

JOEY, REACTING TO GRAY'S THREAT, GRABS HIM BY THE LAPELS OF HIS COAT. THE TWO MEN SCUFFEL. THE SCUFFEL QUICKLY ESCALATES AND GETS OUT OF HAND. FINALLY JOEY PULLS HIS GUN FROM UNDER HIS COAT AND FIRES, ONCE, AT GRAY. GRAY STANDS SHOCK STILL. A BLOODSTAIN, RED AND UGLY, BEGINS TO SPREAD FROM A SPOT OVER HIS LEFT BREAST, SLIGHTLY ABOVE HIS HEART. IT IS AS IF THERE IS A FLOW-ER BLOOMING. GRAY FALLS.

TOM

Oh my God! What did you do? Joey! Jesus, Mary, and Joseph! He's dead.

JOEY

(STILL STANDING WHERE HE FIRED.
THE GUN DROPS TO THE GROUND.)

He got what he deserved. He can't threaten me and get away with it.

(TOM TRIES TO GET PAST JOEY TO
THE DEAD MAN. JOEY GRABS TOM
BY THE SHOUDERS. THAT STOPS HIM.)

There's nothing you can do for him now. What we got to do is get out of here. Out of this town. And fast....

JOEY (cont.)
Tom you go on. Go back and pack our stuff. I'll stay
here and take care of the body. Then I'll get Dopey's
money. We'll catch the Midnight Limited for California.

TOM
Did ya say *we*?

JOEY
Sure I did. You and me are partners, right? We'll
look out for each other. We both need to start a new
life. We can do it out there. So go on.
(JOEY GIVES HIM A PLAYFUL SHOVE)

TOM
(HE STARTS TO TAKE OFF, BUT TURNS
BACK. HE BENDS AND PICKS UP THE
GUN. HE HANDS IT BACK TO JOEY ALMOST
CEREMONIOUSLY. JOEY PUTS IT BACK
IN THE HOLSTER. TOM GRABS JOEY'S
HAND AND PUMPS IT UP AND DOWN.)
This is great. We'll be swell together. You bet.

TOM RUNS OFF STAGE RIGHT. JOEY WATCHES
HIM LEAVE. AFTER A MOMENT, HE GOES OVER
TO GRAY. HE BENDS OVER THE PRONE BODY
AND PUTS HIS HAND ON HIS CHEST.

JOEY
Gray? You OK? You weren't hurt when we
fought?

GRAY
(HE SITS UP)
I'll probably be sore as hell in the morning, but
I'll live. Hey. That wax blood capsule you fired at me

GRAY (cont.)
sure ruined my coat. I don't think this stain will never come out.

JOEY
We had to make it look like the real thing, didn't we? It's a good thing your friendly with that magician guy.

GRAY
That's what poker buddies are for. To give up a few secrets now and again. OK. We got Polanski really scared. Now we have to play our ace. Are you sure you can keep this going?

JOEY
(HE HESITATES A SECOND)
Sure....But, Gray, this kid. He doesn't seem like he's a cold blooded murderer. He's just too nice.

GRAY
Maybe. But he still killed that boy. Even if it was an accident it'll still be a murder. He'll burn for that. Count on it.

JOEY
I guess. But I wish we didn't....

GRAY
Hey, what's this? You going soft on the guy? What's up? You in love with him or somethin'? You turning flitty on me?

JOEY
What! No way! I just was wondering....if it was an accident he might....

GRAY
You just stick to the plan, kiddo. We got him right where we....

THE LIGHTS FADE TO BLACK

A theater is only truly alive when there are people in it. The theater holding *The Greenhouse Murder* was more alive that evening than it had been for many a year.

Originally built as a vaudeville house it had been everything from a church to a skin-flick showcase in its checkered lifespan. Now it was being renovated and restored to become an Off-Broadway Equity Theater. JB's mystery was it's opening show.

Dalton, standing center stage, seemed to be holding his own while chaos reigned freely everywhere around him. The cast members were working on lines and blocking in front of him. The lighting crew had a ladder stage right. The set and costume people were stage left putting together their displays for the investors, who were due later that night. JB was standing next to Dalton with a script in his hand.

"JB, something has to be done about that Joey Swank thing in act three. It's a terrible name. It makes him sound like he's a cufflink manufacturer. You've got to come up with a better nickname for him."

"I know, Dalton. I've been thinking the same thing. But I haven't come up with anything yet."

Overhearing Britt spoke up. "How about Beauty?"

JB turned to face him. "What?"

Toby, standing next to him, turned sideways and spoke to Britt's shoulder. "I told you not to say that."

Britt paid no attention. "Why not call him Beauty? Its basically the same thing and maybe not so awkward."

JB gave it a moment. "Humm....You know, it isn't bad."

"Wait a second." Toby went over to where JB was standing. Quietly he said, "May I talk with you a minute?"

They walked a few steps toward the apron.

"JB, if you nickname me Beauty, and this show goes anywhere, I'm stuck with that nickname for the rest of my career. Please, you can't do that to me. Look what happened to Len with that lousy forelock of his."

"OK. You're right, Toby. But Britt's right too. You are a beauty." JB reached up and touched Toby's cheek.

Toby smiled nervously, then pulled away. He looked toward the rest of the cast members. "Not here, JB. It doesn't look right."

"Oh, sorry." JB pulled himself up straight and became more business like. He raised his voice. "But it's still not right. Don't worry, I'll come up with something."

A sound came from the seating area behind JB. He looked out. "Hello? Is someone there?"

He spotted the figure of a woman standing in the arched entrance at the top of the aisle. She started to come down toward the stage as JB went across the ramp that stretched over the orchestra pit toward her.

"I'm sorry ma'am, but this is a closed rehearsal. Can I help you...."

The woman started to pick up speed as she continued down the steeply slanted aisle. She began to come toward JB at a faster and faster clip. Finally at a full run and a few feet away she totally lost her balance, tripped, then tumbled forward, She was caught before she hit the ground, face down, by JB.

JB, looking at his unexpected bundle said, "Interesting way of meeting people you have there, lady. Is...."

"JB? It's me. Lisa," the bundle said.

JB helped her to stand upright.

Lisa used her hands to straighten her skirt. "It's these shoes. I told Len the heels were too high, but no, I just had to have them. I'm not used to them." She continued putting herself together.

JB, about to speak, stopped in astonishment. He stared at her a moment, then said, "Lisa, you look absolutely lovely."

Post makeover, Lisa had metamorphosed. Her hair, now colored and frosted, was a circle of soft waves. Her brows had been trimmed and elegantly shaped. Her glasses had been removed and she wore subtle makeup which enhanced and brought out the beauty of her eyes. Her mouth, now painted a rich coral, was full and confident. Even her nose, by using expert shading and shadowing seemed narrower.

Her clothing, a Valentino cocktail gown and matching coat, only served as wrapping for the natural elegance she had dug up from somewhere inside herself, captured, and now fully possessed.

"Thank you, JB. But it's all Len's work." She twirled to show off her dress and again lost her balance.

"Maybe you should think about getting training wheels for those heels, Lisa." He helped her stand again. "And where is Len? He's supposed to be here."

At that exactly timed moment Len's voice rang out from the darkness at the back of the stage.

"Hit it, John," Len shouted. His voice went on. "Ladies and gentlemen, Len Matthews Productions proudly presents...."

The house and stagelights dimmed and a spotlight aimed at the now dark stage flashed on and began to move toward the voice. "A Len Matthews extravaganza...."

The light continued across the stage floor until it picked up a set of men's feet. The feet were shod in a pair of light soled grey Gucci oxfords. "Presented by Len Matthews...."

The light moved up from the feet and slowly revealed that Len was dressed in a pale grey perfectly fitted Armani suit. An equally pale grey silk tie lay on a dark grey dress shirt.

When Len's head was caught by the spotlight

he was wearing the hat Dalton had enticed him with the day before. The blood-red band caught the light and burst with dramatic color. Len reached up with an elegant gesture and removed the fedora from his head. The people watching gasped.

His hair, minus the storied forelock, was waved back and plastered down in a perfect twenties hair-style. His hair was also no longer auburn but was now colored pure white. The light caught it and gave it a blue-silver glint.

His eyebrows, also white, ran across his forehead as if bushes on a cliff. Len's eyes were shadowed so they seemed to peer from the valley below. It gave him a slightly sinister look, as if he were wearing a small mask. Above his lip he had attached a small thin Errol Flynn style mustache which followed the curve of his mouth. It too was white.

"So, Dalton....is this what you had in mind?"

Len changed his pose and the red stone of the stickpin glittered from his tie. He had added an ebony and silver topped cane to use as a hand prop.

It was as if, because of the completely grey pallet, he had become a wraith, a specter. A mystery character right out of the dime pulp novels of long ago.

Len returned the hat to his head and lowered his face. The light held on his figure for a moment and then went out. A slight grey shadow shimmered in the now dark space Len had occupied.

Dalton, who had remained still during the entire presentation, now brought his hands together in a single clap. Then another. And another.

He clapped harder and faster as the rest of the people in the theater, even the lighting guy up on the ladder, joined in.

Len came forward as the lights come back up in

the theater and with a great flourish took a deep bow.

Dalton said, "If this doesn't impress the hell out of the investors, I don't know what will." He went over to Len.

"You look absolutely great. Truly wicked. I couldn't have asked for more." Dalton's hand went to the back of his neck. "I swear I feel a hit. I didn't. But now I do." He patted Len on the back. A second later he returned to center stage and picked up the line readings where Len had stopped it.

JB left Lisa sitting first row center and came up on stage to meet Len.

"I am amazed, mon ferré. You went all the way this time, if not a bit overboard."

"Well, you have to admit it's perfect for the play. Gray should be a little heroic don't you think? And it won't hurt to be a smidge over the top. Some of the lines cry out for it. JB, no matter what you might think about my being vain, I am an actor first. And I'll always do what's best for the show."

"I've always known that, Len. I just thought maybe you needed a little reminder." They hugged. "Now, how in hell did you get your hair so white?"

"It wasn't hard. I just had Jose wash out the color I've been using."

"Color? I didn't know...."

"You weren't supposed to, JB. It changed over the last couple of years. With my life the way it was, are you surprised? But this might start a new era for me. Opens up a whole new type for me to play. Distinguished white haired gentleman—Henry Higgins, maybe."

"Or *The Madwoman of Chaillot*."

Toby, released from his scene run-through,

came over to them.

"Len, you look great. I mean really terrific."

"Thanks, kiddo. Where's Lisa? I was supposed to meet her here."

JB pointed in the direction of the orchestra. Len headed that way.

JB turned to Toby. "Uh....do you have any plans for the evening? I was loaned a member card for the Minotaur Connection. There's a meeting tonight. I would like it if you could go with me? It's at ten. At the Puck Building. Downtown."

"Sure, JB. It might be interesting."

"Great. Oops....Dalton is looking for you. I'll see you after he's done."

Toby went over to the group in front of Dalton. JB went to the center of the first row of seats and looked down at Len and Lisa.

"My God, what a pair. I wouldn't know either of you if I ran into you in the proverbial dark alley."

"Looking like this? A dark alley is the last place you'd find us. We're much more the Plaza high tea type."

Lisa looked at Len in amazement. "High tea? I'm more the Playland at the local burger joint. Especially with Susan."

"Sweetie, you have got to get out more often.

"I spend my time at work or at home. After William left I gave up any sort of social life. We still see each other once in a great while because of Susan. But he has a life of his own now, and I'm not in it."

She managed to say this with only a hint of bitterness.

"Well, you're gonna be it now, sweetheart. After I get you out in public tonight I'll bet some handsome deposed prince will hit on you before I can get your coat checked."

She smiled. "Now what would I do with a prince? Any prince."

Len gave her a grin. "I'll help you figure it out, sweetie. You'll know what to do with one who's been deposed. Or reposed. Or even posed naked, before this night is over."

JB sat down next to Lisa. He said, "I did want to ask you something before Len steals you away and proceeds to totally corrupt you." She nodded. "Does your father take any medications on a regular basis?"

Len was incredulous. "Good God, JB. The man is eighty-two. Of course he takes medicines."

"Actually," Lisa said, "he's in quite remarkable shape for a man his age. His doctor says he could go on for years more. He does take blood pressure pills though."

"Well, that has to be the answer. I had a chance to look at Tristen's autopsy report and he had a massive dose of a prescription beta-blocker in his system. That's why he complained of being dizzy before his fall."

"But there was no reason for him to have taken any of father's medicine. I'll have to check but I don't think father has been missing any of his pills."

"Then we have another mystery. Why was Tristen's body full of a medicine he didn't need?"

With the rehearsal over JB went looking for Toby. He found him backstage talking with Britt. They seemed to be in heavy conversation.

Not liking that he must interrupt whatever they were talking about, JB tentatively asked, "Are you ready, Toby?"

"Sure, JB."

Toby turned back to Britt and spoke softly to him. Britt's head bobbed up and down. Toby's went back and forth. Then Toby, with obvious finality, said, "I'll see you later."

Britt nodded, then looked at JB with what he took to be undisguised animosity. Britt then turned around and walked away. As he did he stuffed his hands into his pants pockets. He was clearly in a sulk.

"Something I said?"

"No, JB. We're actors. We have angst." Looking at Britt's retreating figure he added, "Some more than others. Let's get going. OK?"

On the cab ride over JB explained to Toby what little he had been able to find out about the Minotaur Connection.

The Minotaur Group was a loosely organized club of very wealthy older gay men and less wealthy gay younger men. Prospective older members needed to earn at least two hundred thousand a year even to be considered for a limited benefit card. Younger members needed to only have their youth and be attractive.

What drew these two types of men together was mutual desire. What the press insisted on calling "Boy-Toys" and "Sugar-Papas". Younger men or boys who were attracted to older partners and, of course, vice versa. At the Minotaur if that attraction was primarily for money it seldom made much difference to either of the parties concerned. Gatherings were held at various times and places around the City where those interested might come together and mingle.

"So, what this is a barely kosher meat-rack, right?," Toby said.

JB opened the door of the cab and stepped out. Behind him was the Puck Building's Belle Epoch doorway with the small gilt statue of its namesake standing on the ledge above.

"I guess you could call it that," JB said. "They probably prefer something a bit more genteel."

"Like bacchanal?"

Once JB and Toby were in the front entrance a man in formal wear, sitting behind a table, greeted them. On his lapel was a gold pin in the shape of a bull's head, the symbol of the Minotaur. The man checked the membership card JB handed him, then, without subtlety, cruised Toby up and down. The man then reached under the table and pushed a button hidden there. The elevator door slid open. "That takes you to the main hall," he said. "You'll be invested there."

Toby and JB stepped inside, the doors shut and the chamber began to rise.

"Tell me again why we're doing this."

"Because there happens to be some unanswered questions about Tristen's murder plot. There is an ex-lover involved in this. And I need to reassure myself that Harrington Davenport isn't still in any danger from him. So I want to talk to the ex. That's all."

"This isn't just to satisfy some twisted *I guessed who did what to who* thing is it? I know you. I bet this is all just so you can say you were right. You always have to be right, don't you?"

"No, not always. I just prefer the loose ends all tied up and pretty. It makes for a much nicer present."

The elevator doors opened. Before them was a foyer whose walls were draped with yards of white chiffon and tangles of leaves with red berries. Strands of tiny white lights twinkled behind the drapery. In front was a row of white columns with more flowers and foliage artistically wound round. The entrance was through an archway at the center.

Toby laid his hand on JB's arm. "Good grief, it looks like something Laura Ashley coughed up."

"No, not Laura. Even she wouldn't think this was a proper thing."

Once inside, except for more white chiffon on the walls, it could have been the weekly meeting of the local Odd Fellows lodge in any small town in America. A group of prosperous looking men, ranging in age from early middle to very old, stood around in clusters, drinks in hand and talked among themselves.

A man in his mid-forties approached them. He was tall, wearing glasses and a tux, with a paunch showing over the top of his cummerbund.

"You must be new? I'm the Investor. I get to put these on you."

He held up a rainbow-striped ribbon with a gold plated bull's head metal hanging from it. He placed it around JB's neck. Then he moved on to Toby. "Hey, what? Well, hullo there. You are a stunning creature. Are you available?" He placed the ribbon on Toby. Toby stood back a step or two.

"No,: he said. "I don't think so. I'm with him." He pointed to JB.

"Pity. You could do very well here. A bit old for some of the members, but just right for me. You're sure?"

"He said so, didn't he?" JB took Toby's arm and, possessively, pulled him close.

"All right, old top. Don't want to step where I'm not welcome. There'll come a time...."

"But not tonight, old chum." The man started to walk away. "But you could help me. I would appreciate it." The man turned back. "There's a person here I would like to meet tonight. He was the ex-lover of one of the members. Tristen Wispe? I think his name is Billy something."

"Oh, poor Tristen. It's always so sad to hear of someone so young and beautiful being destroyed. Billy is just a wreck over it. He's here. Somewhere. Playing the grieving widow all over the place. You'll know him. He's the one with a black armband and tear streaked cheeks."

The man noticed another set of new arrivals and headed off after them.

There was a ringing sound. It came from a small gong being struck by a little boy. On closer look, the boy turned out to be an adult little person dressed, pretty preposterously, in a gold lamé jeweled turban, vest, and pantaloons, with pointy gold shoes.

As the lights dimmed a deeper ringing gong reverberated. The men in the room formed a horseshoe shape around the edges, facing the far end of the room.

A bank of lights illuminated an elaborate set of maroon colored drapes. They parted to expose a gold colored muscle man. Glistening in the light he wore only a small loincloth to cover his privates. His arm's were crossed over heavily sculpted pecs. On his head was a golden mask of a bull, horns and all. Draped from horn to horn were strings of jewels. The bull's eyes were red stones that glowed brightly in the spotlight.

Then, to the sound of triumphant horns, the Minotaur man held up his arms and spread them open wide. From behind him came a procession of what could only be described as nubile young men. Each was carrying a gold painted papier-mâché cornucopia filled with various fruits. These were fed to the bystanders as they moved around the circle. Cecil B. DeMille's biblical epics couldn't have dreamed it any better. Most of the young men were in their late teens to early twenties. One or two looked like they had just hit the age of legal consent only a few hours before.

The watching older men exploded with wild applause, whooping and whistling, as the boy's pranced in front of them. It was as if a modern beauty pageant had been crossed with a Roman orgy.

"Is this as silly as I think it is?"

"Toby, trust me. It's that silly and more. But it is a pretty clear indication of our culture's obsession with youth. Whether it's straight's lusting after some prepubescent child tap dancer in the Thirties, or gays slobbering over some male model in his Calvin's plastered over Times Square, as a society we have a major hang-up on the young. Its all pretty harmless and shallow usually. Except when some uptight group uses it to justify their particular brand of discrimination. Look at the Boy Scouts. They've taken it so far that I've heard they now have a merit badge in bigotry."

The procession of youths had wound around the room and settled back where the masked golden man still stood. One of the boys then picked up a tray sitting at his feet. Still bowing he held up the tray. It contained various sexual aids—dildos and the like, with a few B&D devices to round out the assortment—sort of a gay tray o' lust.

Grabbing a few of the articles the golden man began to toss them to the men in the surrounding crowd. They grabbed at them as if they were food for the starving peasants.

Meanwhile, his voice, amplified and booming, proclaimed, "I, the Minotaur, open tonight's festival to all gathered here. I invite you, my suppliants, into the labyrinth. There you will suckle at youth's teat and behold its innocence. Wither thou shall search may thy needs be filled!"

He flung open his arms once more and smoke began to billow up and around the platform he stood on.

When it cleared the group of boys and the Minotaur had all disappeared. Also, a second set of drapes had opened to disclose the entrance to what looked to be an elaborate hall of mirrors. The guests crowded into a line and began to enter.

"OK. This has gone around the bend into creepy, JB."

"Well, all the boys have to be over eighteen or the law would step in and shut this down real fast. So, if these grown men want to play at having an orgy, who's to stop them? It does seem a bit over the top, though. I mean a simple cocktail party would serve the same purpose. But men will be children. It's just the toys that change."

"Are we going in there?"

"I don't think so. It's one of those cases where the less we know the better. Let's see if we can find this Billy. That guy said he was here tonight."

"I didn't see any black armbands among the group that went in there, JB."

"Neither did I. Maybe he's up there...."

JB and Toby headed for a set of stairs over on the right of the hall. The stairs led them to the next floor where they found a lounge area filled with leather chairs and couches all facing a bank of windows looking out over the nighttime skyline of the city.

Slouched on one of the couches, holding a drink was a man dressed in an oil black suit. On his arm was a Victorian style black mourning ribbon, complete with streamers. They went over to him.

"Excuse me," JB said. "Is your name Billy?"

The man turned to look at them. He was maybe forty-three but looked as if he was somewhere in his fifties. The drink in his hand was not the first of the evening. It wasn't even the first of the last couple of days. His eyes were red rimmed and baggy, his skin had a yellowish tinge, and his face was jowly and puffy. He had some trouble focusing but once he did he said, "People call me Billy. Why?" He weaved a little while trying to sit up. He didn't suceed so he settled back facing JB.

"Were you the ex-lover of Tristen Wispe?"

The bleary eyes grew watery and began to overflow. He cried loudly. "Oh! Tristen! My baby! My love!" His entire body shook from his sobs.

"I'll take that as a yes then."

"He was my life. I can't go on...."

"I get the point, Billy. You liked him a lot."

"Who are you?" He looked at JB trying once again to focus. "I don't know you, do I?"

"We've never met. But I knew Tristen. Slightly."

"Oh, well, thank you for your sympathy. Now go away. I want to be alone."

"Listen, I was at Harrington Davenport's home the day Tristen fell."

Billy, who seemed about to cry again, stopped when JB said that. He stared at JB, who then continued. "I saw his body smashed and crumpled on top of that car." Billy cringed at that. "My friend here was the one who called the police."

Billy sniffed and said, "Fat lot of good they did. Just like the doctors. The cops can't bring back Tristen and the doctor's can't save me." He looked up at JB. "My liver. Gone." He tried to snap his fingers but only succeeded in sliding one finger past another. "And me with it unless a donor is found. So Davenport wins this round no matter what."

He lifted his drink to his mouth and drained it. "I want another." He started to sit up.

"No," JB said. "You stay there. Toby would you get him a drink, please?"

JB handed Toby the glass

"Scotch and soda." Billy leaned back, then leaned forward to yell at Toby's back. "With a twist." He looked up at JB. "Thanks. Now what do you want? As if it matters." He wiggled around on the couch and finally moved into an even more slouched position with his butt hanging off the front of the cushion. "As if anything matters anymore." His hands rose up and then flopped into his lap again. He groggily focused an eye on JB.

"Well, I'd like to ask a couple of questions about Tristen."

"Like what?"

"Like why did you two break up?"

Billy chuckled as spittle dripped from his slack mouth. "Is that what you thought? Good. That's what you were supposed to think. That was the plan. But Tristen and I were devoted to each other. He was so dear." He wrapped his arms across his chest. "And he loved me."

"He was living with Harrington Davenport. How could you two be together in that situation?"

Billy smiled to himself. "It wasn't what I wanted and I don't care what it looked like. It wasn't so. He was mine. He was always mine."

"So, is that where the murder plan came in?"

Billy looked surprised. "Hey! You know about that?" He waved his hand dismissing it. "Shit. It doesn't matter."

"OK. If it doesn't matter tell me what you two were doing. Why would you murder Davenport?"

Billy made a snorting sound. "Why else? For the money. He had lots. We didn't. We wanted some of his."

"But you belong to this club. That means you have some money. You have to have money to be a member."

"I used to have money." He shrugged. "Now I don't."

"But what about the dues?"

"They get paid if they have too. Sometimes by old friends, sometimes by old...." He waved a hand. "It doesn't matter. They get paid. That's all." Billy waved his arm, sloshing his drink over his lap. "Living like I do isn't cheap you know," he went on. "And finding and taking care of Tristen wasn't easy either. The money went fast. I was about broke when Tristen met Davenport. The old coot fell for him hard. I knew he would. So we made a plan. Tristen would go and live with him then funnel some cash to me. That way we all got what we wanted, and no one was the wiser. And if the old man should happen to die so much the better. He's an old codger. He can't live much longer."

"If that's true, why the murder plot?"

"Because we didn't plan on the old man selling everything he owned. If he did that Tristen would have got nothing. And we couldn't let that happen."

"Obviously you're not aware of it, Billy. But Davenport hadn't named Tristen in his will. He would have got nothing. You wouldn't either."

Billy looked straight at JB, his booze induced fog lifting for a moment. He began to laugh. As his laugh turned to a chuckle he went on. "Is that what you think? That I wouldn't get anything? Well, you're wrong...." He seemed about to say more but stopped. A beat and he continued. "But it's just perfect! Not only did Tristen stand to gain nothing, but now I've lost him too." His laugh had become a brittle cry.

"Billy, I just have one more question I need to ask."

"Well, I have about enough strength to answer one more question. What is it you want now?"

"Was Tristen a drug addict?"

"Huh?" His head shook. "No. He wasn't. There was a time a few of years ago when he had a problem. I had just found him. He was a street kid. I helped him clean up."

"Then why do you think the autopsy found a massive dose of Labetalol in his system? That's a blood pressure medicine. Did he have a problem?"

"Labetalol? That's the same medicine that Davenport takes. Tristen was feeding it to him in the drinks he fixed for him every night. That was our plan. Even prescribed medicine can cause you to die if its taken in large doses. We were making sure his was large enough to finish him off....the old s.o.b. But why Tristen had it in his body I don't know. You don't suppose...."

"I don't suppose anything. It's just a question I wanted answered."

Billy suddenly sat forward in his chair. "Where's my drink? That kid should be back by now."

Billy stood up and unsteadily weaved his way over to the stairway. As he started down he said, "That's it. That's the last question I'll answer. If you have more questions you'll have to find out by yourself. All I know is this isn't how it was supposed to to happen. This wasn't what we had planned. He wasn't supposed to die. Not at all." Billy disappeared down the stairwell.

He's right, JB thought, but he answered everything I wanted to know....except. There was still an answer lurking in a corner of his brain. And it wouldn't come out into the light. I guess it will when I ask the right somebody the right question. Billy was also right about Toby. He should have been back up here by now.

JB also headed for the stairwell and went down.

Toby was standing at the bar, deep in conversation with a man who seemed to have an inordinate interest in what Toby had to say. Or offer, depending on how cynical you were. Under these conditions, in this place, JB could make Gore Vidal look like Pippi Longstocking. The man was leaning in too close, grining like an idiot, listening to every word Toby was saying with predatory appreciation. JB knew Toby could be smart and even witty on occasion, but nowhere near to this degree.

Moving in next to them, JB stood for a moment. When he didn't get noticed he said, "I was waiting for you upstairs, Toby."

Startled, Toby turned to him. "JB." Then he realized what had happened. "Oh, no. I forgot the drink. I'm so sorry. I got started talking here, and...."

"It's OK. We've finished. Billy managed to make it down here and get his own. And who's this?"

"This is Arthur Dell. You know? The agent. We just met." Toby turned to the man, and being the good host, said, "Arthur, this is JB. My....friend."

JB was startled. It was that pause of Toby's

that hurt. JB gave him a look and held out his hand to Arthur.

"Hello. It's nice to meet you. Yes, Toby and I are great friends. Why we're so close you would think we were sleeping together."

Arthur, not an idiot after all, shook JB's hand, handed Toby a business card and excused himself. Turning quickly he headed for the other end of the bar.

Toby looked at JB. If a look would castrate then JB could apply for lead singer in the Vienna Boys Choir.

"That was totally uncalled for, JB." He put Arthur's card in his shirt pocket.

JB reached over and took the card from Toby's pocket. He held it up and tore it in half. He continued tearing it into smaller and smaller pieces. "Was it?" he said. "As good-looking as you are and in this room full of walrus's staking out territory, would you really think I'm not going to do something to protect mine?" He opened his hand and dropped the tiny pieces of the business card onto the floor.

"My looks have nothing to do with this."

"Your 'looks' have everything to do with this. Why do you think these men are trying to steal my claim?"

"I'm not a piece of property, JB. And you're not a miner or a walrus. Although you are acting like an animal." Toby pointed toward the general direction Arthur had gone. "That man happens to be one of the biggest agents in the business. If he shows some small interest in me I'm not going to piss him off by snubbing him. He's a contact, JB. And contacts are what my business is about."

"I realize that. But that man wasn't thinking in

terms of your acting talent. He had something totally different in mind."

"Give me a little credit, JB. I know what he wanted. But if a little innocent flirting on my part can get him to come see the play it might help my career."

"I can think of a couple of careers it might help, however, neither of them are acting."

Toby stared at JB unable to respond. The moment soon passed.

"That really stinks, JB. I've had just about enough of this. If you think I'm going to stand here and listen to you do this to us, you're wrong. I'm leaving." Toby put down his glass. "You know what? You're damn lucky I didn't throw that drink in your face." He turned and walked to the exit.

"Toby!"

JB, belatedly realizing that Toby meant what he had said, followed after him. Just as he got to the archway he saw the elevator doors close. He rushed over and pushed the button. The doors stayed closed.

JB, frantic now, headed for the stairway, slammed open the door, and went down two steps at a time. Pushing through the outside doors he watched a taxi pull away with Toby sitting in its back seat.

As JB watched Toby disappear into New York City's night, his first reaction was to give into panic. Where could Toby have gone? Another club? A friends? The river? Where! Toby's cab could be taking him anywhere, even New Jersey! After he gained control of his runaway imaginings JB hailed another cab and had it take him home. Logic said that was where Toby must have gone.

Logic became superfluous when he discovered that Toby wasn't at the apartment.

Hours passed and Toby hadn't come home during any one of them.

JB waited....

Actually, he had put the time to good purpose by doing some work on his latest book. Another murder mystery.

What made it useful in this particular situation was it provided JB with another world, another place, where he could escape. A place where he could keep control....not at all like what was going on all around him.

His writing had always been a refuge. The one thing he had that never deserted him. It was always there to take him in its open welcoming arms and make him feel better. Lovers might leave, arguments might drive you nuts, contracts might fall apart, people might not be there for you. But the work could always make it go away, like a mother's kiss on a sore elbow. It was a hiding place. It was an entrance into another of life's fine gardens. Where the paths were beautifully laid out, the well-tended plots were in bloom, and all was serene.

Meanwhile, JB's real garden was full to overflowing with cockleshells, bluebells, irises, a rose or two, and that one Goddamned petunia.

Toby seemed to find some source of hurt or anger in everything that JB had done for the last few weeks. And JB wasn't sure if it was his behavior or Toby's attitude that was different. But it did cause for the two of them, if not friction, then major confusion. JB put it down to the stresses of the play. The play was Toby's big break. That sort of pressure could freak out most anyone.

And then there was Len—Mr. Petunia—Mathews. Len going through his first year of sobriety had made for them a friendship that more than pushed the limits of most anyone's tolerance. If it weren't for leftover feelings of love JB still harbored for the guy he would happily leave him to stumble along on his own.

But then, if I must be honest, JB ruminated, I'm not so sure that Len has really benefited from any of the help I have, let's face it, foisted upon him. I would rather call it guidance. He, on the other hand, might call it interference.

And, on the top of it all, like a cherry on the excrement filled sundae that life had felt like lately, there were the unfortunate happenings at the Davenport townhouse. With Len's and Lisa's past relationship a mitigating factor, the only real thing to do was to help them clear up the mess surrounding Tristen's death.

Now that JB knew what the plan was, how the two men were going to kill Harrington Davenport, there was finally a clue as to why one other question had come up.

Or was it actually more than one question?, JB thought. It was clear, even in the condition he was in, that Billy wasn't telling everything he knew. And, there was still that something from this morning in Kelly's office that didn't sit right. It had been knawing at him all day. It was in that autopsy report file. And it wasn't right. But what was it?

After running those thoughts around in his brain a few hundred times JB finally gave up. Answers weren't coming. So, as something to keep his mind from worrying the questions to death, he tried to concentrate on the new novel's nice simple murder as revenge story. He worked until he heard a sound out in the lobby. Then he was up and at the front door of his apartment in moments. When he opened the door Len was just starting up the stairs.

"What are you doing getting home so late?"

Len looked at his watch. "Since it's four-thirty AM, I'd hardly call it late. Early, maybe."

"All right, why so early?" JB stepped outside his door, keeping it open with his foot. "Come on in. Tell me about it."

Wanting Len's company, JB took his seduction a step further. "I have coffee. A really nice French roast. I know its become your main source of sustenance since you went into AA."

Len followed JB's hand wave inside the apartment like an island sacrificial virgin into the volcano.

Len sat on the couch. JB went to the kitchen and poured cups of coffee for both of them. Then he carried them to a fifties coffee table Toby had found one Sunday at the local flea market. He sat.

"OK," JB said slapping his knees. "First, I have to offer multitudes of hosanna's to the miracle you accomplished with Lisa."

"You have no idea."

JB looked at Len with a questioning expression. "I was talking about the make-over. What are you?"

"Oh. The makeover. She does look better, doesn't she?"

"Better? Good God, Len, you took the woman from liverwurst to paté. Better hardly covers it. But what where you talking about? What is it I have no idea about?"

"Idea? Oh, that. Well, you know Lisa and I went out after rehearsal?"

"Sure. By the way, we still have to talk about that number you pulled at the theater. Talk about making an entrance. Couldn't you get the NYU marching band to proceed you? It would have provided the crowning touch."

"I tried. They had some silly game to attend. So I decided on something more subtle. But then the fireworks display didn't go off."

"Well, you still caused quite a stir even without the pyrotechnics. And it is a good look for you."

"Thanks. I was pretty scared at first, but...." Len noticed that JB's gaze kept shifting to the door. "Hey, what's up. Who are you expecting?"

"It's Toby. He hasn't come home tonight."

"Well, JB, he is an adult. He does have some freedom."

"But we argued. And he left me."

"And?"

"No, this was really serious, not just a disagreement. It was a real argument."

"Argument. Tomato. Disagreement. Potato. With you two one is the same as the other. He'll come back. Then talk with him and find out what it is that's bothering him."

"No, Len. Talking a problem out is what you and I used to do. Toby won't communicate. If I try to bring up something that he doesn't want to discuss. Something simple. Like what the hell is wrong with our relationship? Well, you could probably wring a better answer from the Mona Lisa. Toby just sits there refusing to respond. It's maddening."

"And that drives you nuts, right? It always was a way to get to you. What you need to do is put the frustration aside and work past the wall of silence. Use a battering ram if necessary. You know the man hiding back there. That was the guy you fell for. You just have to get back in touch."

Len patted JB on the leg. A moment passed. Len cleared his throat. "Now, can I be selfish? I want to turn the focus on me for a moment. I have a huge problem."

JB smiled. Guidance. Interference. One's the same as the other. Especially when it's asked for. "OK. Be selfish. What?"

"Well, you know Lisa and I went out tonight?"

"You said that. So?"

"We had a wonderful time."

"Mazaltov."

"Did I mention that years ago, at acting school, when I was still confused, I had a huge crush on Lisa?"

"Just a second....You had a crush on a girl? You were confused."

"There was a time when I wasn't sure I was gay."

"When was that? A Tuesday in March of Nine-teen-Forty-eight?"

"JB, this is serious."

"I'm sorry, Len, I was just confused. OK, how does a crush from your obviously indecisive past apply to seeing Lisa in the here and today?"

"JB, we spent the entire day together. From eight this morning until just a little while ago."

"And?"

"And, we had a wonderful time. I can't say it better than that. She and I were like this great couple. Like Nick and Nora in *The Thin Man* movies. It was really scary. Both of us were on exactly the same wave length all day. It was Lisa that helped me make the decision for this new look. And then she talked me through it while it was done. And I did the same for her. We supported each other, JB.

Then later, after the rehearsal, we had a terrific time. We went night clubbing, JB. I didn't know you could still do that in New York. You have got to go to the Rainbow Room someday." Len handed JB a program from the club. "It was out of another old movie. She was like Rosalind Russell and I got to be Cary Grant. After we had an early breakfast at this all-night diner in her neighborhood. Dressed for night clubbing, JB. Is that out of an MGM picture or what? Then I walked her home. We stood on her stoop and talked some more. We kissed goodnight. Then we slept together. And after that I came home...."

"Wait just a second there, Lenfield. You did what?"

"Oh, God. We slept together, JB. That's right. You heard me. Lisa and I had sex. Together. And, yes, you can laugh if you want."

JB didn't. Len went on.

"That's it, JB. We made love. And it was.... I can't describe it, JB." Len was wringing his hands together. "It was good, JB. I mean really good. It felt like our bodies were fashioned by an artist expressly to fit together like we did. It was...." Len shook his head. "Wow....just wow."

"And, this is the problem? I mean, so you slept with a woman. Gay men have done that before."

Len faced JB squarely.

"No. That's not it. Just sleeping with her isn't the whole story." Len hesitated a moment, then went on. "JB, I think I've fallen in love with her. Actually in love. Madly and deeply. I mean the whole thing. I want to marry her, and have a kid—just one, because there's already Susan. But I want one of our own.

"Hold on there a second, fella." JB shook his head. "They told me this could happen, but I didn't believe them."

"Now, what are you talking about?"

"When you and I were having problems in our relationship. You remember, don't you?" Len bobbed his head. "Well, I went to some Al-Anon meetings. At one of them they told me that often when a gay person gets sober they will decide they're straight. Suddenly, after years of being gay, they are convinced they want to find a woman, marry her, and become a card-carrying breeder. I didn't believe them." JB threw up his hands. "Silly me."

"Well, what's wrong with having a family?"

"Len, you're gay. If you have any family, it's a gay family. Believe me, I know, you're gay."

"Don't be so quick to judge. I could be bi-sexual."

"In this case I would call it try-sexual. Len, I lived with you for a few years. We were lovers. I think I'm in a position to have inside knowledge. You're gay."

"You adore raining on people's parades, don't you?"

"No, not really. But life isn't always a *Macys* Thanksgiving parade either. You can't have floats and clowns every moment. Sometimes you have to let reality take first place."

"I think I like it better with the floats and clowns."

"And you think you're not gay?"

Len left soon after.

JB continued waiting for Toby.

After fifteen minutes JB found an old blanket, lay down on the couch, and slept.

At the sound of the key in the door JB was awake and sitting up. His watch said it was just after eight A.M. Toby came in and switched on the light. He looked none the worst for wear. No visible wounds, anyway. He wore the same clothes he had on last night, although they were a bit more wrinkled now. His hair was damp and combed flat.

"Oh, JB. You startled me. What are you doing here?"

"Everybody's gotta be someplace." JB stood and began to fold the blanket that had covered him through the morning. "Toby, a better question might be, where were you? Where the hell did you disappear too? I've been here all night....hoping you were all right."

"I'm fine. I went to a friend's."

JB went over and pulled Toby into his arms. "I'm just glad you're OK," he said. JB stepped back then and looked into Toby's freshly shaven face. "And you had sex. With this friend, I suppose. Who was it, Toby?"

Toby, completely taken by surprise, blurted out. "But I took a shower after...." He stopped. When he realized what he'd said he tried to re-group. "JB, we didn't do...."

"Don't try to lie your way out of it, Toby. I can sense the other man on you. Every person has his own particular odor. You're friend's odor isn't the same as mine. I can tell the difference."

"What the hell are you? A cat?"

"Every animal can tell his own scent. Even the human animal, Toby. I can smell the man you were with.

And plain old soap won't wash it away."

Toby, as an actor, should have had better control over his emotions. His face first showed arrogance. That quickly changed to fear. He then moved on to embarrassment at the whole situation. Softy, he said, "It was Britt. That's who it was. I was in the cab and angry as hell at you. I reached into my pocket and I found a napkin with his number. So I called him...."

"The kid from the show? Well, at least he's closer to your own age. That's better than most of the men from last night."

"You always go to the age thing, don't you, JB?"

JB went to the couch and sat. "Oh, my God. Do you really think this is nothing more serious than an age difference."

"JB...."

"Toby, don't you understand? This goes right to the foundation of our being together. It goes directly to trust, Toby." JB shook his head. "I don't feel like I can trust you anymore."

"But, JB. Please. It was a one time thing."

JB looked up. His face was flushed. And sad. "How can I know that? If you can be tempted once. And you were going to lie about it." His head moved back and forth. "Toby, this is our lives we're talking about here. There's an epidemic going on. Too many thousands have died already. So far I've been lucky. I won't take a chance that it won't stay that way."

"JB, I was safe. I know that."

"But I don't. And that's the problem. Toby, when we first got together we made promises to each other. Right? Do you remember?"

Toby reluctantly said , "Yes."

"That we would be monogamous. I have been. Now, you've chosen not too. And I can't know if this is even the first time. Have you lied to me before? You see Toby. That's what I mean about trust. I just can't trust you anymore."

"Oh, JB. No." Toby's voice was shaky from his effort not to cry.

"Toby, I think I might take the empty apartment up on the second floor for awhile. I think we need to spend some time apart."

"JB, you can't just take your stuff and move on, like some Arab nomad. Here one second and gone the next. We can work this out."

"And, I'm sure we'll try to work it out. But I don't think it's a good idea for us to be living together right now. You and I aren't a good match right now. I'm really more angry than you realize. And I am profoundly disappointed in you."

JB stopped and looked over at Toby. An unasked question hovered in his head. He decided to ask it.

"Toby, I don't understand. How could you do this to our relationship?"

"I....JB, it's just that you were such a total shit last night, I had...."

"OK. I was acting too possessive. I'm aware of that. But, I just can't get used to someone as beautiful and desirable as you choosing to stay with me. So I tend to go a little nuts when I think I might lose you. But this, Toby. I would never go this far. To break one of the main promises of our relationship. That's way over the line. I think you and I have some things to work on because of this. And being away from each other right now is a good way to start. It will give us room to think."

Toby had tears running down his cheeks. He'd lost that battle. Maybe he could still win this one.

"JB, please. I don't know how to convince you. I don't want you to leave."

"But I have to, Toby." A tentative smile moved his lips. "Toby, it'll be fine. Well, not fine, but OK."

JB carried the folded blanket to its place in the hall. He paused at the closet door. He let the ache in for just a moment. Then he went back to the living room where Toby was still standing; still stunned by the turn their lives had taken.

"Hey, don't you have a rehearsal this morning?"

Wiping his face, Toby said, "Oh, hell. Yes. Damn. I don't want to leave it like this, JB."

"It's all right. Go to your rehearsal. I'll move a few things upstairs. Then I have to go to the Davenport's later. When I finish there we'll have dinner, OK? Then maybe we can talk. I mean really talk."

"OK. But it's the tech today. They always run late. I don't know when I'll be through."

"I can wait."

Toby grabbed JB in a tight hug, then kissed the side of his face.

JB put his hand to the side of Toby's cheek and, in a familiar gesture, ran his index finger along Toby's jaw, stopping at and touching his lower lip.

Toby grabbed at the hand and held it against his face. JB could feel the wet from Toby's tears gathering in the hollow of his palm.

Tech rehearsals are when sets, costumes—every element that has to do with a theatrical production, including the actors, all come together for the first time on the stage. All of this bringing together has to have some meaning, so every piece, every tiny particle, is tested to see that it works.

Most tested were the actors. The cast would begin with their first lines at Act One-scene one and continue on until they reached the end of the play.

In theory this should have been a simple and quick procedure. What interminably held up the proceedings, and made tempers raw, were the waits and endless stops needed to make changes....adjust the lights, move scenery, adjust the lights, change the drape of a costume, move an actor or prop....

which to the crew were the same thing....adjust the lights, re-block a scene so actors going off-stage didn't run into actors coming on-stage, make sure the props were in the right place, and then adjust the lights once again.

Furthermore, you might have to change a too pale makeup on an actor so it would read better, repeat the scene over, and then over again, to get the light or sound cues correct, and then there were still more lights to be adjusted.

It was mid-afternoon and the cast had worked their way to the beginning of Act II.

Dalton was sitting fifth row center with his ears stuck in a headset that was tied to the lighting booth. The cast was standing in place so the light crew could move another light another fraction of an inch.

Len, standing on stage next to Toby, said, "I saw JB earlier today."

"Before or after I got home?"

"Before. Why?"

"Then you're not up on the latest. JB is moving out."

"Out where?"

"Out of our apartment, Len. We, or rather he, decided we should live apart. We're no longer a live-in couple."

Len shook his head. "Uh-uh. No. That isn't right. I'm sorry, Toby, but I know JB. He won't give up on any relationship this easily. He may move out, but he won't leave your life. He'll be around for this and the next millennium."

"Well, we are supposed to have dinner later."

"There. You see. But if you want my advice....and even if you don't, here it is....you need to open up to him, kid. Tell him how you feel. JB prizes honesty above everything else in a relationship. I learned that early on....something to do with getting in too late from a business meeting. Hey, it was my story and I'm sticking to it. Anyway, if he knows you're not trying to bamboozle him he'll listen to anything you have to say."

"Bamboozle?"

"An old Southern word for not trying to flim-flam him."

Toby was more confused. "Flim-flam?"

Len rolled his eyes. "It's the same as bamboozle. Oh, never mind. Just be honest with him, Toby. If he's wrong he'll admit it, but....and here's the hard part....you have to do the same."

Dalton yelled from the seats out front. "All right, cast. Let's continue. And Len, can I get a little more life to your lines. You sound like you're asleep."

"You would sound asleep too if you were being forced to play this silly game of yours. What's it called? Oh, yeah, check the lights three hundred and fifty eight times and drive everyone currently standing on the stage up the proverbial wall. I suspect this is a childish and mean-spirited revenge thing you have going on here."

Len stepped to the stage apron defiantly.

Dalton was up and walking toward the stage. "We just want your pretty face lit to its best advantage, Len. The new sets have meant a new lighting plan." He leaned his elbows on the apron. "If all of you will be good little mannequins this will go much faster."

"Dalton, how can you stand yourself? It must be difficult knowing how really annoying you are as a human being."

"Annoying, maybe. But I'm not the legendary bitch

queen around here."

Len had started to turn away, but stopped at Dalton's remark. His body whipped back.

"That's it, you toad!" Len was crimson. "I'm leaving." Len stomped over to the side curtains, stopped and looked back. "You're damn lucky I'm not a violent person, Dalton Hughes, or I'd rip out those hair-plugs on your forehead and put them back where they harvested them from....on your ass!"

He walked off the stage, followed by astonished laughter from the rest of the cast. Dalton was up on the stage and going into the wings after Len in a flash.

That left Toby and Britt, still standing center stage, to fend for themselves.

"I was hoping we could talk some more, Toby."

"Britt, since you're the reason my relationship is currently in the dumpster I don't have a whole lot to say to you."

"Uh, Toby. Reality check. I wasn't the one who broke his promise to his lover. I can't break what I don't know about. I'm sorry, but you screwed up, Beauty. I just had sex with a hot man."

"Thank you for your support," Toby said.

Dalton caught up to Len at his dressing room door. "Len, I'm sorry. That remark was totally wrong I shouldn't have said it. You're not a bitch queen."

Len turned to face his now apologetic accuser. "Dalton. Damn it. Of course I'm a bitchy queen. I was hypnotized by a George Sanders movie when I was just a toddler. Then throw in my being an actor, and that I'm gay, and you're bound to get Addison DeWitt by way of Cliffton Webb!" Len's shoulders dropped. "Oh, hell, I can't do this anymore. I hate these bitchy remarks I always come up with. The problem is I don't know how to stop doing it. I think them and out they go. Zing. A Minuteman inter-continental ballistic missile should have as good an aim as I do. I don't know how to stop it. Then, Dalton, you have to go and announce it right in front of the whole company. Now that was bitchy."

Dalton threw back his head and laughed. "But, honey, why would you want to change? It's gotten you this far, hasn't it?" Still laughing he threw his arms around Len, pulled him roughly to him and tightly hugged. "You know, sometimes being a bitch is what keeps you going when everything else fails. Going straight for the jugular keeps the jackels from eating you alive. Besides, Len your remarks have taken on a life of their own. I hear them repeated all over town. The jungle drums are probably sending that last one out over Broadway right now. And I'm loath to admit this, since I've been at the epicenter of several of your better zingers, they're funny. I bow to the master."

He leaned his head forward and looked into Len's face. And kept looking.

"A life of their own, huh?"

That's when Len realized he was still trapped in Dalton's arms.

"Uh, as nice as this is, Dalton. Don't you think you should let me...."

Dalton kissed Len. It was the sort of kiss that mixed real adoration with a soupcon of actual lust.

Len stood perfectly still with his eyes open. He

wasn't exactly sure what to do. Should he break it off and slap the man silly, or....

A moment later Len felt an ember somewhere inside him begin to ignite. He was surprised to find himself responding to Dalton's adore.

Now their tongues were on a search and discover mission. Each of the now clinging men were putting in as much effort as the other. Each of them was trying to lose the same battle. The war that raged between them was momentarily forgotten in the heat of the skirmish.

Dalton finally broke their kiss when he ran out of air. He gasped for a breath and looked at Len. "I'm so glad I finally did that. I've been wanting to kiss you for weeks. It just seemed so romance novel cliché.

Len laid his head on the door behind him. "I like romance novels," he said.

Dalton wiped at the sweat on his forehead. "My....Uh....that was...."

Len heard the hesitancy in Dalton's voice. He opened his eyes. "Yeah, wasn't it." He gave Dalton a fake punch to his shoulder. "Well, I guess that settles that."

"What?"

"You, Mr. Hughes, have reminded me why I'm gay. That's all."

"Glad to be of service."

They walked arm and arm toward the stage.

"You know, Dalton, this is going to make it quite difficult to hate you from now on."

It was late afternoon and JB had once again walked the few blocks over to the Davenport's street and townhouse. He took the steps to the front door and rang the bell. Emma, efficient as always, answered the door.

"Ah," she said. "It's you is it? Well, you'll be welcome I'm sure. Come in."

JB asked after Harrington and was told that both he and Miss Lisa were in the library. He started in that direction but then changed his mind. He turned to Emma and said. "May I ask you a question or two about all that's been going on?"

She squared her shoulders. "I told that Kelly person the other day what I saw."

To combat her combative stance JB put on his most ingratiating smile. "Actually, that isn't what I wanted to ask about."

"What then?"

"Well, Emma, Mr. Davenport said you've been with them for quiet a long while."

Suspicious, she said, "Yes, sir, that's correct. I came to this house with the first Mrs. Davenport."

"That long ago? My, you must have been through so much with this family." He clucked his tongue with sympathy for her fortitude. The expression he used on her he hoped would turn hard stone to malleable clay.

"Yes, sir, that's true. I've been with this family for all its up and downs....and all it's shame too, if I must be honest." Her mouth pursed, expressing her considered judgment on the foibles and foolishment's of her employers.

"I'm sure. How difficult it must have been to see all that and be unable to do anything." JB's shook his head in understanding. Emma now seeing JB as her ally let down her guard. JB had become her confidant.

"Oh, and awful it was to see. Poor Mr. Davenport was devastated when his son, Mr. Brett, was killed. And it changed this family completely. Not necessarily for the better, I say. But that's all I'll say on the matter. Except that Mr. Davenport is to this very day, taking that boy's death hard. Putting all his money into that foundation. To cover his own guilt, I say. He should have been closer to that boy. But it's not my place to judge. And Miss Lisa. What a trial she's been, defying her father like she did. To be an actress of all things. Then getting married, and that against here father's wishes too. What do they say about an ungrateful child? Then dragging dear little Susan back here when she couldn't keep her man. It's a good thing Mr. Davenport is so forgiving, I say, or she wouldn't have it so good now. But, he's gotten old, and he can be foolish, bringing that Tristen riff-raff to this house. Why, if I had my say...."

JB interrupted. "So you think Mr. Davenport brought Tristen here as a replacement for his son?"

"Oh, Tristen may have looked the same, but he wasn't anything like Mr. Brett. Mr. Brett was brilliant. Tristen was an uncouth piece of baggage. Tristen replace Mr. Brett? Never."

Emma again pursed her lips trying to decide if she should say more. She did.

"That Tristen was a user, Mr. Bent. Him and that ex of his. Billy. They worked together, I say."

"Actually, I met and spoke with Billy the other night. It looks like you're correct in your assessment. They did have plans to murder Mr. Davenport."

Her hand went to her mouth.

"In hopes of getting his money."

Her hand dropped. Her lips again were compressed tightly. "It's always the money, isn't it?"

"By feeding him poison."

"The scoundrels. But I'm in charge of all of Mr. Davenport's meals and medications. How could they have poisoned him?"

"By feeding him extra dosages in a drink Tristen served Mr. Davenport each night."

Emma again gasped.

"Were you missing any of Mr. Davenport's blood pressure medicine?"

"I'll have to check."

"He takes Labetalol, right?"

"Yes, that's the medication. He's taken it for many years. It's a beta-blocker. Its meant to slow down the heartbeat."

"And an overdose would slow it even more. Since he already took it they didn't think it would be detected after he was dead. At Davenport's age a too slow heartbeat would kill him quickly."

"I knew that boy was up to something. I just didn't know what. Miss Lisa approved his making the drink for her father. I didn't like it, I must say. But I didn't say anything, it wasn't my place."

JB went on. "But the most interesting part is that it was Tristen who ended up with the poison in his system. His autopsy showed a large concentrate of the drug. And you know what, Emma? I suspect that Mr. Davenport somehow had figured out what Tristen was up to, and I think he switched the drinks when Tristen delivered them. That way he fed the overdose to Tristen and not himself. What do you think?"

JB smiled to himself. *And Len thinks he's the only one who can schmoose. He should see this* performance.

"Oh, my," Emma said. "Mr. Davenport did that. What must he have been thinking?"

"Well, he is pretty old. He might not have realized the consequences of his actions. How serious they were."

"That's possible. But he did give the poison to the man who was trying to kill him. I might have done the same."

"Then you would have been committing a crime, Emma. Just as Davenport did if he fed the medicine to Tristen. Don't you think not drinking it and calling the authorities might have been a better option?"

"Oh, Mr. Davenport wouldn't have called the police. In this house we prefer to take care of our own problems without outside interference."

"I see. You know Emma, there are rumors going around that Mr. Davenport's foundation is in financial trouble. Is that what the auction was all about? Taking care of their problems in-house?"

"Actually, JB...."

He turned and discovered that Lisa was standing behind him. He hadn't heard her approach.

"....there are no real problems," she continued. "I haven't driven the foundation into bankruptcy as the rumor mongers would have it. Father was simply selling off several of his acquisitions to avoid taxes at a later date."

"Lisa. I didn't know you were there. How much did you hear?"

"From about the time you accused my father of killing Tristen." She looked at Emma. "Would you prepare a tray for tea," she said sharply. "Right away."

Emma nodded and went toward the hallway and the kitchen. Lisa turned to JB with an anguished expression.

"He couldn't have, JB."

"Everything points to it, Lisa."

"But he's eighty-two, JB. He couldn't survive what the police, not to mention the media, would do to him over something like this. We've got to protect him. Will you help, JB? Please."

They walked toward the library.

"I would say the first thing to do is to find out if my theory is true. Then we can figure out what might help."

The doorbell rang. Lisa stopped and looked back. "Now who?" Emma, a towel in her hands, reappeared at the hallway entrance and started for the door. "Emma will get it." She escorted JB into the room where her father was waiting.

"JB!" Harrington moved toward the pair. "I'm so glad you came today. You must stay for cocktails. The doctor hates that I have my drink every night, but it's my last vice. And I refuse to give it up." He put his hand on his daughter's arm. "Isn't she lovely? I just can't get over what your friend has done for her." With obvious pride, he said, "She's glowing. And so beautiful."

JB nodded and said, "You know, Len was pretty surprised himself at what he was able to accomplish. It had been years."

"Years? What does that mean?"

Lisa had the courtesy to blush. "Nothing Father. JB just means Len hasn't done anything like this in a long time. Makeovers, I mean."

"Exactly," JB said.

JB and Lisa exchanged a glance. A throat c

cleared itself behind them. Emma was standing in the doorway.

"Excuse me, Miss Lisa. But that Lieutenant Kelly is here again. From the police. He'd like to see Mr. Davenport."

"Send him in, Emma." Lisa worriedly turned to JB. "I wonder what he wants?"

In every play there is a moment when the action stops and the actors stand pregnantly waiting for the next performer's entrance.

Kelly walked gingerly into the room. His size and build made him feel like a Grizzly bear, all lumber and clumsiness, among the antiques that furnished the living room. He made his way past the French chairs and German figurines with a careful tread. Once seated on the couch he said, "I'm sorry to bother you, Mr. Davenport. But a couple of things have come up that we need some clarification about."

"Anything I can do to help, Lieutenant."

Kelly reached down and opened his briefcase. He pulled out a folder. JB recognized it as containing Tristen Wispe's autopsy report.

"Kelly, you good police person you. I was hoping you would have that."

JB went over behind Kelly and reached over his shoulder to help him leaf through the contents.

"I think I can do this on my own, Bent." Kelly pulled out a sheet of paper.

"If that's all you need? May I look at the rest?"

Kelly held up the folder, which JB took from him. JB then moved over to a Louie the something chair and slouched down into it. He began to read.

Kelly, in his standard pit-bull mode, growled his questions at Davenport and Lisa. "Now, this is a report that states that Tristen Wispe had an unusually large amount of Labetalol, a controlled substance, in his system when he fell from your balcony. Do you have any idea how that happened?"

Lisa, standing behind her father, placed a protective hand on his shoulder. "How could we have any idea, Lieutenant?"

"Now, Lisa," Harrington said. He was about to continue when JB interrupted.

"Lisa, didn't you tell the Lieutenant that Tristen had a history of drug abuse?"

Kelly turned to look at him.

Lisa stammered, "Uh. No. I didn't."

JB went on. "At least that's what I found out last night. Lisa, I know you did say you were going to ask your father if any of his medicine had gone missing? At the theater?"

Lisa nodded.

"I would have no idea about that sort of thing. Emma keeps track of all that," Harrington said.

Kelly turned back to face Harrington. "Then I think I'd like to speak with Emma. Can you have her come in?"

"Of course, Lieutenant." Lisa went to the pull beside the fireplace.

Emma opened the door a little too quickly, making it clear how she knew so much about the family.

She stepped in. "Yes, Miss Lisa?"

"The Lieutenant would like to ask a question, Emma."

"Of course, Miss."

Kelly stood to face the housekeeper. "You keep track of Mr. Davenport's medication, do you?," he said.

"Yes, sir."

"Were there any amounts missing lately?"

"Missing? I don't...." She stopped and looked directly at JB. He looked back, his expression a studied blank.

"Well, sir. I just this moment checked through my old records. We always receive Mr. Davenport's medication in three month increments. The last order that came only contained two months. I didn't think anything of it then. I just ordered another from the pharmacy."

Kelly said, "That must have been it. Tristen must have taken Mr. Davenport's drugs for his own use."

Lisa spoke up. "We did tell you he had complained of dizziness, didn't we, Lieutenant?"

Kelly nodded. "You say you have a record of the missing drugs? I'll need to see that."

"Emma will be happy to show you, Lieutenant."

Kelly picked up his briefcase. "If those records check out, I've got what I came for. We know where the drugs in his system came from, and we know he fell from the animals bite on his ankle. I can't arrest a little dog for nipping at a heel. It's what dogs do. It was simply an extraordinary accident. Well, that closes the case. Uh, Bent...."

JB looked up.

"Are you finished with that?" Kelly held out his hand. JB closed the folder, stood, and handed it to Kelly.

"I'm done with it," JB said. "I found what I was looking for. So, you have all that you need? You won't be doing anymore investigating?"

Kelly nodded. "If the records check out."

Emma, standing at the door, coughed. Kelly looked over. "Yes, OK. I'll be right there." Kelly thanked everyone and followed Emma out.

Harrington was the first to speak after he left. "I'm not exactly sure what happened here, but I'm glad the case is closed." He looked at his daughter.

"Father, I have to ask this. The cocktail that Tristen used to bring you every night....did you switch the glasses so Tristen would drink it?"

Harrington sat back in his chair. "He didn't make them right. Too much vermouth. They tasted wrong. I didn't want to hurt his feelings so I switched them. His for mine. I didn't realize...."

Lisa went to him and kneeled beside him. "All right, father. It's all right." She looked up at JB. "That's the answer then." She turned back to her father.

"Yes, I guess so. At least that part of it. But what I read in the autopsy report brought up another question. Is Susan at home?"

Lisa's head snapped up. "Why? What do you want her for?" She stood, her stance clearly indicating she would protect her child at all costs.

"I just want to talk to her, Lisa."

"Well, I guess you can. But I'm going to be there too. She's in her bedroom. Down the hall...."

"Third door. I remember."

With Lisa hovering close behind him JB stopped at Susan's bedroom door. He raised his hand to knock when the front doorbell chimed.

Lisa, impatience coloring her voice, said, "Now who is that? JB, don't go in yet. I want to see who this is."

She turned and started to walk toward the front, stopping at the archway to the foyer. Emma came out of the kitchen door and headed for the front.

When she opened the door Len stepped in and began to ask for Lisa. He spied her standing in the archway, skidded around Emma, and went directly over to her.

"Lisa, I have to talk with you...." JB walked up

to the couple. "Len, what are you doing here? You're supposed to be at rehearsal."

"I took an early dinner break. But I have to stay late working on that last scene. Some problem with the body mike. I needed to talk to Lisa. So I'm here. And you?"

"Me? I'm just cleaning up some questions concerning Tristen's fall. In fact, why don't you and Lisa have your talk while I go in and speak with Susan?"

Lisa started to object. JB interrupted. "I just have a couple of innocent questions to ask. It'll be fine, Lisa."

"All right, JB. But you had better...."

"I understand completely." JB turned and headed down the hall.

Lisa turned to Len. "All right, let's talk. But not here. Let's go out on the terrace." Lisa then turned to Emma, who was still standing in the foyer. "Emma, you were making tea weren't you? Bring it out there, please."

Emma nodded and went to the kitchen.

Lisa took Len's hand and led him through the hallway entrance to the balcony. Leaning against the iron railing, she lifted one leg and rubbed at her foot.

"Now what did you want to talk about, Len?"

"First, what's with the foot thing? You look like a lawn ornament."

"It's these shoes you made me buy. They hurt and they're too high."

"But, sweetie, they make your legs look fabulous. And looking fabulous was the point, right?"

"I suppose. But what I didn't realize was that fabulous was supposed to be this painful?"

"Sweetheart, if you look in the dictionary,

under painful it says 'see fabulous'. So until fashion decides that hospital orthopedic style is what's in and attractive this season, you'll just have to suffer." He shrugged. "But your foot problems aren't why I came here."

"Yes, Len, what did you want to say?"

"About last night."

Lisa smiled. "Yes? What? I have no complaints."

"Well, Lisa, I have to tell you....I mean I need to.... Oh, hell, regardless of what happened last night, I'm gay."

"Yes."

"I don't think you get it. You need to understand.... as terrific as last night was. And it was terrific, by the way."

Lisa nodded. Len grinned.

"Lisa, I'm a gay man and I always will be."

"Len, don't you think I know that? I understand completely. I know you're gay. My God, Muggsie knows you're gay."

"Then you're all right with a one time thing?"

"What I had last night was a delightful experience with a very dear man. A man who was gentle, loving, and managed to make me feel that I was desirable. A facet of myself I had quite forgotten. Thank you, Lenfield."

She leaned forward and kissed his cheek, then wiped the lipstick she left behind.

"Oh, my Lord. Am I never going to live down that first name? And what do you mean Muggsie knows?"

JB, inside Susan's room, found her sitting on her bed, a book in one hand, and Muggsie, the alleged ball of murderous fluff, lying comfortably in the crook of her other arm.

The pet, sensing JB's alien presence in her space, bared two rows of pointed teeth and began issuing a five-second warning growl.

When that time had elapsed the growl became a single bark. Then Muggsie was out of her mistresses arms and pacing along the edge of the bed, obviously protecting the borders of her territory.

JB's still refusing to retreat caused Muggsie's single bark to escalate to a series of high pitched yips and grievously agitated jumps along the now, in her opinion, breached battlelines.

Susan, now up on her knees, grabbed at the little animal. But Muggsie wriggled away from her grasp and quickly approaching rabidity continued her tirade.

Susan then swung over and reached into her nightstand drawer. She pulled out a box of dog treats, and tossed the box over to JB.

Grabbing several treats, he held them at arms length and dropped them in front of Muggsie. She quickly snatched one and retired to a safe place beside Susan. She chewed on the treat with the same fervor as her previous attack.

"Ah-ah," JB said. "So she can be had for a couple of *Liver Doodles*."

Moving over to Susan's desk, JB took a seat on her small cushioned chair. His knees riding close to his chin he looked the desk over and spied a delicate silver frame holding a picture of a man. JB picked up the frame and asked, "Who's this?"

"That's my Daddy. I see him one weekend a month. That's what the courts will allow."

"And do you or don't you like that?"

"I really don't care one way or the other. Daddy is fine. He buys me presents and things. And he takes me places. Probably because of guilt. At least that's what they said on Oprah."

Susan seemed to be a child who was quite precocious. Mature to the point of about forty-three.

"Susan," JB said. "I'll be honest with you. I have one question to ask you, and then I'll let you get back to your reading. What is that you're reading anyway?"

Susan held up a copy of Erica Jong's *Fear of Flying.*

"Ah, research?"

"Is that your question, sir?"

"No, Susan, that wasn't it. Actually the question is about your little dog, Muggsie. You two didn't like Tristen very much, did you?"

"That's your second question. But, no, we didn't. He said some really bad things. He wasn't nice like your friend Len. You got a second question, that means I get to ask you a question."

"OK. What do you want to ask?"

Without hesitation she said, "Is your friend going to marry my mother?"

"Would that be a bad thing?"

"That's your third question. You don't count very well do you? I like Len, but mother doesn't know him very well. He's gay, you know?"

"Honey, everyone knows. Except Len. He just thinks he's theatrical." Susan giggled. "But to answer you, no, Len and your mother won't be getting married. But they are friends. And you can't do better than to have Len as a friend."

Susan held up Muggsie and nuzzled the little animals nose.

"Then that's all right. They must be pretty good friends though. You should have seen them last night. Kissing each other and everything."

"You saw that? I know...." JB held up his hands. "That's another question. Well, Susan, I think you can be pretty sure that kind of kissing won't happen again. Now, will you tell me exactly what were the bad things that Tristen said?"

JB backed out of Susan's room pulling the door with him as he did.

Hearing a metallic sound he turned to see Emma weighted down by a cumbrous looking silver tray. It held a silver teapot, matching cream and sugar bowls, porcelain cups, a plate of what smelled to be fresh baked scones, and a tub of marmalade. She looked at JB. There was a question on her face.

"Susan is going to take a nap. I turned down the light and left the door ajar."

"Ah." Emma put her tray down on a table. "Then I'd better go in and check that she's comfortable."

JB bent over the tray, savoring the baked goods. "These scones can't taste as wonderful as they smell."

"Keep away from those. You'll find out when I bring them to the terrace. Although, that Kelly person seems to think his are pretty good. He hasn't growled once since I put them in front of him."

"He and Muggsie are alike that way. Both can be had for a snack. You said the terrace?"

"That's where Miss Lisa and your friend went. I'm to serve out there."

"Then that's where I'll go."

Walking out onto the terrace JB found Len and Lisa standing together. Before he could get across to join them Lisa said, "Is Susan all right?"

JB nodded.

"What did she tell you, JB? I have to know."

"Lisa, she was very helpful. She told me that she and Muggsie didn't like Tristen very much. It was exactly what I needed to know."

Lisa's face went pale. She grabbed onto Len's arm with a grip that, judging from his suddenly pained expression, was not gentle.

"She also told me she heard what Tristen was saying on the phone the day he fell. Tristen wasn't very discrete it turns out. He said that he was going to hurt Susan's grandfather."

"Oh, no," Lisa moaned. Len's expression turned to agony as he pried each of Lisa's acrylic enhanced fingernails from digging into his arm.

"That would have been just about the time that you saw Susan bite Tristen on the ankle, right?"

A shocked Len looked at Lisa.

"You saw what? Hey, wait a minute. That phony faint. It was to draw attention away from the balcony. So we wouldn't see Susan out there."

Lisa nodded. "Now do you understand why I

couldn't explain?"

JB continued. "While we were attending to you Susan left the terrace and went to her room, taking Muggsie with her. Those two are seldom apart. It stands to reason that if Muggsie was on the balcony then so was Susan. Right?"

"Right," Lisa answered. "But how did you know it was Susan and not the dog?"

"That's what I was trying to remember."

"Remember?"

"From the autopsy pictures. It was the bite mark on Tristen's ankle. The mark didn't look like an animal bite. It was the wrong shape. What it looked like was a human bite. A small bite for sure, but definitely human. So it had to be Susan that bit Tristen."

Lisa sighed. "I saw her through the window. It happened so quickly. She ran over, grabbed his leg and bit him. When he started to lose his balance Susan was already leaving the terrace. I don't think she even realized what she had done."

"Well, Kelly has closed the case so I see no reason to get it re-opened just to implicate a little girl. Or an old man."

The three stood silent as Emma came out onto the terrace with the tea tray.

What Emma, or any of the others, hadn't noticed was that Muggsie had left her mistresses room and followed behind Emma and the scent of the fresh scones. The pet hunkered down in the hall and waited for a crumb she could snatch.

Emma set the tray down. Lisa's waved her hand dismissing her. That left Lisa to take over pouring duties. As she sat before the service tray the protective mother demeanor she had previously exhibited was replaced by a gracious hostess mode. She even managed chatty.

"JB, I am so glad you've decided to let Susan's involvement in this go by. I don't know what I would have done. It's such a relief to know the police won't be bothering us any longer." She held a cup out to Len. "And, of course, father's involvement too. Do you want lemon, JB? I mean I can see how you figured out he could be held partly responsible for Tristen's fall. Cream? Especially after you talked to Billy. But father is just so frail of late." She handed over JB's cup. "I don't think he could have withstood the questioning that would have been involved. So I just want to thank you for your help." She held out the plate of scones.

Muggsie, out in the hall, sat up.

JB carefully set down his cup and reached into his pocket. He pulled out the small silver-framed picture from Susan's room and held it toward Lisa.

"I had meant to ask you about this later. I was interested in what you would say. But, now I think I'm going to have to mention it to the Lieutenant. So, Kelly still won't be bothering Susan or your father but you'll be seeing him quiet a lot."

Len sat forward while taking a scone from the plate. "What is it, JB?"

"It's a picture, Len. Of Susan's father. Lisa's ex-husband."

"Oh?"

"And Tristen's ex-lover."

"Huh!"

"I think Lieutenant Kelly will be very interested to know that your ex-husband and Tristen's ex-lover were the same person, Lisa. You see I met Billy last night."

Lisa shrugged her shoulders. "So? My gay husband left me. How would that interest the

Lieutenant in any way?"

"On the surface, maybe not very much. Unfortunately, in a world that forces men and women to fit into little boxes built only for probity's sake gay men marrying straight women happens more than it should. On the other hand, I am sure the Lieutenant would be very interested in how Billy came to know just what type of man your father would be interested in forming a relationship with. And how Billy just happened to be a member of the same club as your father, even though he admitted he was broke and couldn't pay the dues. The Lieutenant might also be interested in how Billy was able to take Tristen....a 'street kid' as Billy called him....clean him up and make him presentable, so he could conveniently meet an old man who just happened to have a dead son he looked exactly like. How long did it take you two to find him, Lisa?"

"I don't believe this. What are you implying?"

"I'm not implying anything, Lisa. I'm out and out accusing. Last night Billy kept saying 'we'. 'It wasn't what we planned.' I thought he was talking about Tristen and himself. I was wrong. He was talking about you and him. You two were the *we*. I'm accusing you of collusion, Lisa. Between Billy and yourself."

"Collusion? My goodness, that's just too droll." She waved her hand as if the idea was simply a gnat that was bothering her. "Len, really, teach your friend some manners. How rude can a person be. After all, Len, you did bring him into my home. And now you let him accuse me this way? Collusion? Absolutely ludicrous."

But Len was looking at Lisa with newly jaundiced eyes. "You know, Lisa, when JB puts it like that. I mean with Billy being your ex? And Tristen's too? That's a pretty hard coincidence to swallow."

"What? You too? I don't understand this. How could you both jump to this idiotic conclusion? It's ridiculous. Absolutely ridiculous." Lisa stood, as if ready to leave the terrace. JB stopped her with his next question.

"Lisa. How did you know I spoke to Billy?"

She turned to face him. "What? I don't...."

"You said it just a moment ago, 'especially after I talked with Billy'. The only way you could possibly know I had talked with him is if you also talked with him. He must have told you about our discussion of last night."

Lisa just stared at JB.

JB went on. "And another piece of the puzzle fell into place when Emma told me that you had approved Tristen's serving your father his evening drink. Against her better judgment, she said. You were perfectly aware of what was in that drink, weren't you? You just didn't know your father was feeding it to Tristen instead of drinking it himself. That must have come as quite a shock."

Lisa had been standing in front of JB taking each accusation he threw at her like a stab from a knife. She found herself unable to catch her breath and felt as if she might faint, for real this time. She swayed and reached out again for Len's arm. He pulled it away.

JB slowed his attack when he said, "So, Lisa, how are you going to answer me? What kind of fake faint or bogus bluff are you going to try now?"

In a voice with no bluff left in it and it's timber rising in direct proportion to her desperation, she said, "But why? Why would I even try?"

"I can only make a guess, Lisa. Maybe there is some truth, despite your denials, to the rumors about the Davenport Foundation being in financial trouble."

"But I told Len, I'm just a salaried employee of the foundation. What could I do?"

"As the director you have access to the funds, Lisa. What I'd like to know is what would happen if the foundation's books were subjected to an audit?"

"Father wouldn't allow it. He would...."

Harrington, who had been standing quietly in the shadows of the doorway to the terrace, stepped forward.

"Don't fool yourself, Lisa," Harrington said. "I would not only allow it, but will demand an audit be conducted beginning first thing tomorrow morning."

"But father, how can you? With your cash gifts coming in and those huge sums going out. With your approval. Always with your approval. You can't possibly keep track. And the board. They won't approve an audit. The expense."

JB kept lobbing accusations at Lisa. He became relentless in his effort to break her, to make her confess.

"Your father may have approved of the foundation's expenditures, but I don't think you approved of your father's generous policies very much. Did you, Lisa? How you must have hated watching all that money slip away. And you couldn't do anything to stop it, not while he was still alive. But when he's gone, Lisa? When he's dead and buried in the cold hard ground. What then? As his only surviving family member you stood to own every grubbing penny of it. All of it would then be yours."

Lisa had shrunk back, covering her face with

her hands, as if to ward off any lightening bolts angry gods might rain down on her.

JB went on. "Once he was dead, Lisa, you would have it all. You could cover any current foundation shortages on the books and clear yourself. Then later, when the board had elected you CEO you could quietly disband the entire operation. Then you'd be left with all the money not used by then. Very sweet, Lisa. But the nagging problem was Harrington's.... how did you put it?....'Remarkably good shape for a man his age'. He is old, but he won't die. And you won't get your share until he is, right, Lisa? So how much were Billy and Tristen supposed to get for their contribution to your murder scheme? How much was your father's life worth to them, Lisa? How much was it worth to you?"

Harrington's voice was now shaky and stricken. King Lear couldn't have felt more betrayed. "Is that what you had planned, Lisa? Were you going to kill me? Please, tell me it isn't true. You can't wait the little time I have left? How long can it be?"

Trapped, Lisa shouted at her father, "While you squander every cent we have on these ridiculous centers of yours? They're useless. And stupid. They serve no earthly purpose."

"If they give one boy or girl shelter after being thrown out of their house by parents who won't accept them for who they are. If they help one gay youth find others like himself so he doesn't feel alone. If they give pride to one lonely homosexual. I think that's doing quite a lot."

Fuled by all the rage held inside for years Lisa's voice dripped with hatred and venom. "That, my dear old fool, is a total crock. Those centers are there for one reason only. Too absolve your own guilt over Brett's death. You've held on to that guilt for years. But it wasn't my fault, old man. Why should I lose millions because you couldn't tell your own son you were a fag? It isn't fair." Lisa's voice had risen to a high pitched screech. Risen almost to a tone only dogs could hear. The exact tone dogs found irritating as hell

Muggsie, still hunched outside the terrace door, had her head cocked to one side. Her ears were raised reacting to Lisa's hysteria. She decided to take action.

She barked. A rapid fire high pitched yipping meant to warn everyone within a five foot radius of her displeasure. When her warning wouldn't stop the source of her irritation she hunkered down on all fours, growled, and shot out onto the terrace aiming directly for the noisemaker.

Muggsie reached Lisa and in an instant had barked, growled, and leaped up onto her legs several times. Her angry barks increased in volume. Her claws dragged and scratched, putting run after run in Lisa's hose, and leaving red welt's on her legs.

"Get down, Muggsie!" Lisa shouted and slapped her hands at the animal. "Stop it,"

One of Lisa's slaps connected with Muggsie's snout. She stopped leaping, but hunched down and began to growl in earnest.

Lisa, no longer paying attention, turned to JB. Her face was white with anger and she yelled at him at the top of her voice, "Damn you. You just had to be so damn smart, didn't you?" She took a step toward him, her arm up-raised as if to strike him.

Muggsie had stopped her growling and now attacked. She sprung at Lisa's right leg. Lisa's ankle being several inches off the floor because of her high-heeled shoes made grabbing Muggsie's usual target difficult to reach. So, Muggsie decided to go for the next best thing, She bit at what she was able to reach. She chomped down on the leather heel of the shoe itself. Her jaws locked and she rocked her little body back and forth at the same time pulling backward. A deep growl punctuated each pull. Lisa took several steps back.

JB gave Len a push. "Go help her, Len."

"Not me, Sport, I almost lost a finger to that beast already. Let her save herself."

JB found himself unable to move to her aid. He was marveling at the tenacity of Muggsie. The little beast refused to let go of her prey.

Lisa, reacting to the force of the dog's attack had taken several more steps backward, dragging Muggsie along with her. When the balcony railing touched the small of her back she stopped. Balancing on her left foot she then lifted her right, with Muggsie still hanging by her clamped teeth to her heel. Shaking her right foot Lisa tried to dislodge the animal.

Not immediately succeeding, Lisa kicked out her foot, causing Muggsie to sway back and forth like a clock pendulum. Another kick only caused the dog to sway more. She looked at the three men standing watching her. She shouted, "Well do something for God's sake!"

JB said to no one in particular, "Where the hell is a *Liver Doodle* when you need one?"

Completely exasperated Lisa kicked her dog held right foot once again. And then again even harder. That's when the edge of the tile that had been keeping Lisa's left shoe steady to the floor stopped holding. Her left leg flew into the air. Muggsie also picked that moment to give up the fight, and loosened her grip on Lisa's other heel. Muggsie dropped to the tile deck.

The three men—Harrington, too old to move over to help her quickly enough; Len, still gun-shy from his previous encounter with the animal; and JB, shocked into inactivity by the quickness of the little dog's attack—found themselves standing silent and still, in awe as this tableau played out in quick moments in front of them.

Lisa, now with no weight to balance against, both feet off the terrace tiles, and only the balcony railing holding her, choose this moment to inexplicably give one more solid kick of her right foot. It was just enough force to tip her backward and propel her body over the railing.

Harrington gasped. "Oh God! No!" He watched as Lisa's very chic and fashionable high-heel shod feet disappeared from his view.

Her scream could be heard diminishing in volume as it went faster and further from where just seconds ago she had stood fighting a small orange ball of fluff.

Muggsie, the ball of fluff, shook her body to right her fur, barked once at the now empty spot where Lisa had stood, then turned and padded toward the terrace door.

Lisa's scream stopped abruptly and was replaced by a car horn's steady wail. When JB, Harrington, and Len looked over the railing they could see Lisa lying on her back, her open dead eyes looking up from the same crumpled automobile roof Tristen Wispe had lain in just days before.

"Did I hear a scream?" They all turned to find Lieutenant Kelly, a scone in his hand, at the hallway entrance to the terrace.

THE GREENHOUSE MURDER
ACT III, scene 4

THE LIGHTS COME UP ON A HOTEL ROOM CEN-
TER STAGE. THE HALL DOOR IS TO STAGE RIGHT.
A CONNECTING DOOR TO THE NEXT ROOM IS ON
THE OPPOSITE WALL. THE NEXT ROOM IS DARK.
THERE IS A DOOR TO A BATHROOM ON THAT WALL
AS IF THE TWO ROOMS SHARE A BATH.

A BRASS BED IS AGAINST THE BACK WALL BE-
TWEEN TWO WINDOWS. A DRESSER AND MIRROR
STAND BETWEEN THE BATHROOM AND THE CON-
NECTING DOOR. A CHAIR, TABLE AND LAMP ARE
ON THE HALL WALL.

TOM IS PUTTING THE LAST FEW ITEMS INTO A
VALISE ON THE BED. HE CLOSES IT, THEN SETS
IT ON THE FLOOR NEXT TO ANOTHER BAG.

JOEY ENTERS THE ROOM FROM THE HALL.
HE CARRIES WITH HIM A SMALL BAG SIMILAR IN
SHAPE TO A DOCTOR'S BAG.

JOEY
(HOLDING UP THE BAG
FOR TOM TO SEE)

JOEY (cont,)
I got it, Tom. Our ticket to freedom.
TOM
Great. This'll be our chance. We can use that money to make a killin' out in Hollywood. Did you get the tickets for tonight?
JOEY
You bet, partner.
(JOEY PATS HIS BREAST AND THEN WALKS ACROSS THE ROOM AND OPENS A DRAWER TO THE DRESSER)
Hey, didn't you leave out a clean shirt for me? I got to wash up.
TOM
I'm sorry, Joey. I was so excited I just packed everything.
JOEY
It's OK, kiddo. I can wear the same shirt.

JOEY MOVES ACROSS TO THE BED AND TAKES OFF HIS JACKET. HE HANGS IT ON THE BEDSTEAD. IT IS POSITIONED SO A WHITE TICKET FOLDER SHOWS FROM THE JACKETS INSIDE POCKET.

JOEY ROLLS UP HIS SHIRTSLEEVES AS HE GOES INTO THE BATHROOM. THE SOUND OF WATER RUNNING AND JOEY SINGING AN OFF-KEY DITTY DROWNS THE NOISES OF TOM'S ACTIONS.

TOM SPOTS THE TICKET FOLDER IN JOEY'S JACKET. HE CROSSES OVER TO THE BED AND SITS. HE TAKES THE FOLDER FROM THE POCKET AND OPENS IT UP. HE READS IT. THEN HE RUNS HIS HAND THROUGH HIS HAIR, SHOCK AND SURPRISE CLEARLY SHOWING ON HIS FACE. HE STANDS AND

BEGINS TO GO TOWARD THE BATHROOM BUT
STOPS. HE TURNS AND GOES INSTEAD TO THE
CHAIR WHERE HE SITS HEAVILY.

THE WATER STOPS RUNNING. JOEY COMES
FROM THE BATHROOM DRYING HIS HANDS. NOW
WHISTLING THE SAME TUNE. TOM IS UP FROM
THE CHAIR AND MOVES TO STAGE CENTER TO
CONFRONT JOEY.

TOM
(HE HOLDS THE FOLDER
TOWARD JOEY)
You planned on going to California alone. There's
only one ticket.
JOEY
Well, kiddo. How do I know you won't rat me
out?
TOM
Joey, I'd never do that. Don't you get it? I love....

JOEY CROSSES QUICKLY TO WHERE TOM IS
STANDING. HE RAISES HIS HANDS, PALMS OUT.
TOM CRINGES, AS IF AFRAID. JOEY PUSHES TOM
BACKWARD BY PLACING HIS HANDS ON HIS CHEST
AND SHOVING. TOM STAGGERS BACK SEVERAL
PACES. JOEY FOLLOWS HIM. WHEN THEY ARE
CHEST TO CHEST JOEY PUTS HIS HAND OVER
TOM'S MOUTH.

JOEY
(HE SPEAKS IN A FRANTIC VOICE)
Don't you say that. Don't you ever say that!

JOEY MOVES HIS HAND FROM TOMS MOUTH AND PUTS BOTH HANDS TO HIS CHEEKS. HE CONTINUES TO HOLD HIS FACE. THEY STAND LOOKING AT EACH OTHER. THEN TOM RAISES HIS RIGHT HAND, SLOWLY, TENTATIVELY. HE TOUCHES JOEY ON THE WRIST. JOEY MOVES HIS HEAD BACK AND FORTH TWICE. THERE IS A SMALL SMILE ON HIS LIPS. HE THEN LEANS IN AND KISSES TOM GENTLY, TENDERLY, ON THE MOUTH.

TOMS RESPONSE TO THIS IS GRABBING HOLD OF JOEYS HANDS AND HOLDING THEM TO HIS FACE. TOM LEANS INTO JOEY, LOOKS HARD INTO HIS EYES, AND THEN KISSES HIM, HARD.

FOR A MOMENT JOEY LETS HIMSELF GO AND KISSES TOM BACK WITH THE SAME PASSION.

THEN ABRUPTLY HE BREAKS IT OFF. JOEY STANDS BACK. HIS HANDS ARE STILL HOLDING TOMS FACE. JOEY SHAKES HIS HEAD AND THEN LET'S HIS HANDS FALL AWAY. HE WALKS PAST TOM TO THE DRESSER AND STANDS WITH HIS BACK TURNED TO TOM.

JOEY
(HE LEANS BOTH HANDS
ON THE DRESSER)

Tom, I trust you today. But suppose someday we quarrel. You might run straight to the coppers and tell them that I killed that man in the park.

TOM

No, I wouldn't. I couldn't. You got to trust me, Joey.

JOEY

Tom, why should I trust you? You got a hell of a weapon to use against me. I can't let you have that.

THE LIGHTS BEGIN TO RISE IN THE CON-
NECTING ROOM.

A MAN WITH A STETHOSCOPE IS HOLDING IT
AGAINST THE CONNECTING DOOR. A SECRETARY
IS SEATED A SHORT DISTANCE AWAY FROM HIM
TAKING DOWN WHAT THE MAN IS REPEATING TO
HER.

STANDING BEHIND THE SECRETARY IS GRAY
AND A UNIFORMED POLICE CAPTAIN.

TOM
(HE CAN SEE THEIR PLANS
GOING UP IN FLAMES. HE
HAS TO STOP IT)

I know, Joey. If you have something on me then
we're even, right? It'll keep us both honest. Joey, I
did it. I killed a guy too.

JOEY
What? I don't believe you. Who did you kill?

TOM
That boy. The one the guy you hit was talkin'
about. The kid at the greenhouse. We was playin'
around, you know, with each other. He started to
hustle me. When I wouldn't pay he was gonna tell
what we done. I couldn't let him do that, so I hit him.
On the head.

THE LIGHTS BEGIN TO FADE AS TOM CONTIN-
UES TO CONFESS HIS CRIME.

GRAY
(TO THE POLICEMAN)

GRAY (cont.)
Is that what you need?

THE POLICEMAN NODS.
THE LIGHTS DIM TO DARK ON THE ENTIRE STAGE. THAT LEAVES GRAY VISIBLE IN A SINGLE SPOTLIGHT. HE PUTS ON HIS HAT AND LEANS HIS HEAD DOWN. THE BLOOD RED OF THE HATBAND GLOWS WITH A NEON BRIGHTNESS IN THE SPOT.

GRAY
(HE WHISPERS. BUT IT ECHOES
THROUGHOUT THE THEATRE)
Vengeance!

THE SPOTLIGHT HOLDS ON HIS FIGURE FOR A MOMENT AND THEN GOES OUT. A SLIGHT GREY SHADOW SHIMMERS IN THE DARK.

CURTAIN

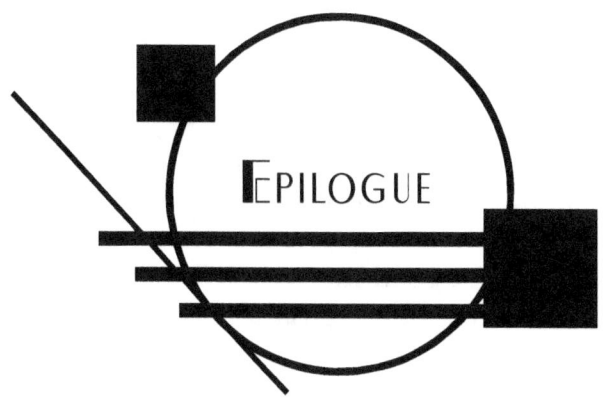

EPILOGUE

As they each in turn took their bows, the opening night applause washed over the cast of *The Greenhouse Murder*.

Toby got a noticeable rise in volume, a tribute to his budding charisma. Len got a few Brava's, a tribute to his new look, his guts, and his undeniable talent. Dalton was applauded wildly, a tribute to his reputation. Then Len and Toby had dragged JB out to the center of the stage where he heard the words *Author* and *Bravo* together as one sentence for the first time. Even if he recognized the voices as a couple of friends it was still the nicest kind of tribute.

Later, after an hour or so of the opening night party, JB finally got a chance to sit with Len and Toby and fill them in on his conversation with

Muggsie will be put down as a mad dog."

"Does PETA know about this?" Len said.

"And I might point out that Muggsie had nothing to do with Tristen's fall, Susan did it," Toby added.

"That's for Susan and her therapist to work out over the many of what I'm sure will prove to be provocative and fascinating sessions. Wouldn't you like to be a fly on the wall for those?" JB smiled.

That's when Dalton came through the front door holding a stack of newspapers. He shouted, "Here we go, kids. We got good money reviews from the TV stations. Let's see what the papers say."

The critics called it a "modest entertainment" and "not a whodunit but a how-to-catch-em". So *The Greenhouse Murder* wasn't a smash hit. But the decent reviews were enough to convince the investors to move the show to a small Broadway house as soon as they could. Having Harrington Davenport as your behind the scenes angel didn't hurt either.

Meanwhile the rumor of the move to Broadway kept the Off-Broadway ticket sales brisk enough so the show ran in the black week after week.

Toby wouldn't be going to Broadway with the play. It only took three performances for a movie studio producer to see his possibilities. The producer just happened to have a part that was a perfect fit for someone like Toby.

Toby, happily gathering contacts again, asked to arrange for the producer to buy out his contract

Harrington Davenport that afternoon.

"So," JB said. "He changed his will. After he's gone Susan will get everything, but not until she's twenty-one. Until then the foundation will serve as executor and Emma will be her guardian."

"I assume he did the audit," Len asked.

"Yes, he did, and it showed that Lisa had set up a fake community center and then overfunded the hell out of the sucker. That was how Billy was able to afford his lifestyle with Tristen. She made him the director of the fake center with a salary larger than what Imelda Marcos paid for all her shoes combined. But that expensive lifestyle has finally come back to bite him on the butt. Actually, another organ. He's checked into Lenox Hill Hospital with a liver that is so overworked it's on the brink of failure, and he hasn't a chance in hell of surviving the wait for a donor to get him another."

Toby said, "Then in the final analysis all the bad guys end up dead by accident or illness, and the good guy gets to die a natural death. Somehow that doesn't work out."

"True," JB answered. "But life often just ain't fair. At least one person might turn out mostly sane from this mess. Harrington has put Susan into daily sessions with a therapist."

"Because of losing her mother?"

"That's partly it. But it's mostly because she is completely grief stricken over having Muggsie taken away from her."

"I assume the police have the little beast," Len said.

JB nodded. "At a shelter. A judge has to decide if the animal is actually responsible for both Tristen's and Lisa's deaths. If he decides she is with the play.

That made any future JB and Toby might have had as a couple seem pretty unlikely. Toby in California making contacts and JB living in New York was a much bigger problem than any of the others they had to face. And JB wouldn't let Toby pass up a chance at a movie career.

With Broadway now looming in Len's future, he was dreaming of having a musical career. To that end he had secretly started taking singing lessons.

JB had started to get some little tentacles as feelers from the West Coast about the script of Greenhouse. It was a gamble, but he thought he'd wait until it opened on Broadway to decide. If it worked there the price would skyrocket. If it was a bomb then JB would just have to write something else. Maybe a novel about an attempt on the life of a rich man by his lover and his lover's ex-lover.

About the author:

Ken Lansdowne has lived in California, Nevada, New York City, New Mexico, and now lives in Denver Colorado.

The Fairy Dust Killings is the third novel in *The Bent Mystery* series.

The first novel in *The Bent Mystery* series is *Secrets Don't Belong In Closets*, the beginning. Second is *A Murderous Ball of Fluff.* *The Fairy Dust Killer* is the third. Fourth is *Home Sweet HoMo.* Fifth is *Dance:Ten Murder:Maybe?.* Sixth is *A Mystery, Wrapped In A Mystery, Surrounded By A Mystery.* Seventh is *The Art Of Death,* and number eight is *Bathhouse Bloodbath!*

There is also a Gay themed Christmas novella: *Jacob Marley*

If you would like to get an automatic e-mail when the next book in the series is ready for release sign up at k.lansd@outlook.com. Simply put the word "LIST" in the subject line of your email. Your e-mail address will never be shared and you can unsubscribe at any time.

Word-of-mouth is crucial for any author to succeed. If you enjoyed the book please consider leaving an online review, even if it is only a line or two: it would make all the difference and would be very much appreciated. If you didn't like it I apologize for taking up your time: my purpose was only to entertain or give you a laugh or two.